BEST FRIEND AND OTHER ENEMIES

MY BEST FRIEND AND OTHER ENEMIES

CATHERINE WILKINS

nosy crow

First published in the UK in 2012 by Nosy Crow Ltd
This edition published in 2019 by Nosy Crow Ltd
The Crow's Nest, 14 Baden Place, Crosby Row
London SE1 1YW, UK

Nosy Crow and associated logos are trademarks and/or registered
trademarks of Nosy Crow Ltd

Text © Catherine Wilkins, 2012
Cover illustration © Joel Holland, 2019
Interior illustrations © Sarah Horne, 2012

The right of Catherine Wilkins to be identified as the author of this work
has been asserted by her in accordance with the Copyright, Designs
and Patents Act, 1988

15

A CIP catalogue record for this book is available from the British Library

Printed and bound in Great Britain by Clays Ltd, Elcograf S.p.A.
Typeset by Tiger Media

Papers used by Nosy Crow are made from wood grown in
sustainable forests.

ISBN: 978 0 85763 095 7

www.nosycrow.com

For Rich, Kim, Suzy and Duncan.

Thank you.

C. W.

CHAPTER 1

"OK, Jessica, we're going to McDonald's now," says Natalie as we all get off the school bus in town.

"Great," I say.

"No," sneers Amelia. "*We're* going to McDonald's now. Natalie and me. You're not invited."

I feel like I've been slapped in the face. I'm suddenly worried I might cry. I won't cry. I'm too angry to cry.

"You don't *own* McDonald's, Amelia," I retort. "It isn't invite only. You don't exactly need to RSVP to get in."

Amelia sighs and rolls her eyes. I hate Amelia. Natalie, my supposed best friend since Year One when we shared finger paints, shuffles her feet

1

awkwardly.

"The thing is, Jess, Amelia and I need to talk about something," says Natalie.

"Something private?" adds Amelia, in a tone that suggests I am a tiny child.

"You don't mind, do you?" says Natalie. "We'll go to McDonald's another time. Just you and me. Yeah?"

Checkmate. I can't argue with that. Well, I can – but not if I want to maintain the dignified moral high ground.

"Oh, OK. No, of course," I say. I do the new fake smile I've been practising so much lately. "Have fun, you crazy cats!" I slightly shout. Then I turn and start walking towards my house. (Crazy cats? Wish I hadn't said that. That's just given them something else to laugh at.)

My throat feels tight, as it often does whenever Natalie and Amelia tell me they are going off to do some new thing together.

I briefly wonder about doubling back and turning up at McDonald's anyway, and saying, "Oh, this is a coincidence!" and then they'd have to let me join

them. But (a) I have no money, and (b) I have *some* pride. Some.

What has *happened* to Natalie? Honestly, what has happened to her? We used to do *everything* together. And it was brilliant.

Now it's like she doesn't even *remember* the time we made a den in her living room (with bedsheets) and sat in it all night eating Fizzy Wands and looking for ghosts with our torches; or the time we decorated these T-shirts with matching rainbows and pretended we were in a new kids' pop band called Scoop (I don't know why we did that now, but it was really fun).

And she *never* used to ignore me like this. She was always there for me, *always*.

When my mum read that report on the dangers of E-numbers, and banned me and my brother from having chocolate for two weeks (she gave us fruit for school break time instead. Fruit!), Natalie brought in an extra Club bar for me every day.

Natalie's always been so awesome. But since

Amelia's joined our school, it's like she's a different person.

Anyway. I don't need them. I can amuse myself. Plus, I have plenty to get on with at home. Plenty. Like … well … I mean there's … well, for instance … um. *Hmmm*. OK, that's not a good sign.

What did we all do after school, before Amelia came along and convinced everyone that McDonald's is the *place to be*?

Well, Nat and I were quite outdoorsy and we used to spend a lot of time in the park. We used to go really high on the swings, and sometimes we'd play It and British Bulldog with the other kids in the neighbourhood. Sometimes we made dens in the shrubbery. But Amelia didn't think that was a very glamorous activity.

Honestly. Amelia arrived here six months ago and has been nothing but trouble. (In my opinion.) I mean, everyone else seems to think she's quite cool. But that's because she hasn't tried to steal *their* best friends away.

Not that she's succeeded. Natalie and I are still best friends. Well, kind of. We *are* still best friends, but we just hang out less. But anyway, the point is,

4

I'm brilliant. It's just that no one realises.

I haven't been home long when there's a loud crash outside my bedroom window. I get up and look out. My mum has just tripped over the assortment of toys my little brother always leaves on the front lawn.

As I look out, my mum is picking herself up and the crashing noise subsides and is replaced by shouting. She starts furiously waving a red fire engine in one hand, and a blue space hopper in the other. I catch snippets of "black bin liner … I mean it … warned you so many times …"

My dad opens the front door and ushers her inside. He speaks in much more hushed tones, so I can't hear what he's saying, but I imagine it's something along the lines of "don't need the neighbours to hear".

My parents are quite into keeping up with the Joneses. The trouble is that the Joneses (or, in our

5

case, the VanDerks) are quite a lot better at most things than us.

Their front lawn is much greener, and doesn't have any dandelions or daisies (or toys) strewn about on it. Their children, Harriet and William, learn musical instruments – properly. They actually practise and seem to care about it. Harriet is in my year, though she's in the parallel class, and she's top of practically everything.

The VanDerks' house is just much more serene in general. Harriet and William don't seem to run and shout as much as Ryan and I do. (Or my older sister, Tammy, who's left home already, sometimes did.) And their car is much cleaner.

My parents sometimes mock them behind their backs for being obsessed with cleaning their car, but to their faces they are almost sickly sweet.

I remember when the VanDerks got a new surround-sound system, because they left the box it came in outside their front door for a week. My dad scoffed that they had obviously done this just so that we would see it and be jealous, and that they should be embarrassed for being so showy; but I think the real reason he was upset was because their surround-

6

sound system was better than ours. (The box of which we'd left outside for a week the month before.)

Honestly. Sometimes I think adults can be very immature. I'm eleven, and you don't catch me getting into petty rivalries like this. Well, except maybe with Amelia, but that is not really my fault.

Amelia is *much worse* than the boring old VanDerks. The VanDerks don't tell me my jacket reminds them of the time their sister was sick on the dog. And they certainly don't invite Natalie over for the weekend, but not me, and then go on about all the popcorn and chocolate ice cream they are going to eat while watching 15-certificate films, right in front of me. I mean, if the VanDerks *did* do that, I could understand why my parents were bothered by them.

The front door slams and I hear what my mum's shouting more clearly. "Ryan? Ryan! Are you even listening to me?"

Poor Ryan. He's only six; it's not his fault. He's always in trouble. I mean, I know he can be quite boisterous, but that's just the way he is. It's almost like my parents have decided that he does it on purpose or something.

"Oh, I'm overreacting, am I?" My mum is obviously responding to my dad's efforts to calm her down. "Tea? That's your answer to everything." (That's true; my dad is very pro-tea.) "All right, fine. If you think tea is so brilliant, I *will* sit down." I pause, waiting for any more shouting. No, that does seem to be the end of it. Phew. Well done, Dad, with the tea.

Don't get me wrong, my parents are lovely people. Lovely. But they are especially lovely when the world is neat and tidy and everything is going well.

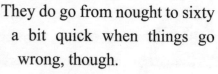 They do go from nought to sixty a bit quick when things go wrong, though.

I become aware of an odd noise. My phone is vibrating somewhere at the bottom of my bag. I dig it out and see I have a new text message from Natalie.

Hi eaten 2 much ice cream I feel sick LOL. UR better off not cumin. CU 2moz! X

I don't know what to make of this, but I am spared wondering for too long, as my dad starts shouting up the stairs. "Kids! Dinner!"

Ryan and I open our bedroom doors and look at each other. Ryan is wearing his space helmet.

"All right, my little astronaut?" I say. Ryan smiles shyly and nods.

We go downstairs, Ryan hanging back a bit, not sure if he's still in trouble. I walk along the hall and Ryan tiptoes behind me like a ninja.

I open the kitchen door, and my mum completely ignores me and shouts, "Ryan! Come here, love. I'm sorry I shouted at you. Give me a hug, poppet."

Ryan hugs my mum, his space helmet bashing her in the chest and ribs. She winces in pain but lets this go.

"Helmet off, please, Ryan," says my dad, who is already seated at our kitchen table.

"But I'm a spaceman," says Ryan.

"Off. You're lucky your mum's forgiven you. You were very naughty leaving your toys everywhere again. You are in no position to negotiate."

I don't think Ryan knows what the word negotiate

9

means, but he does know he was just in trouble and so probably shouldn't kick off again too soon, so he takes his helmet off and sits down obediently. He starts chatting away to my dad about how good he is at rounders, as if there's been no row at all. I wish I could get over being upset as quickly as Ryan.

"Jessica, love, will you thank Lisa for the flowers when you see her? So kind of her," says my mum.

Lisa is Natalie's mum. Last week, Natalie and I planted some purple tulips and white anemones in my parents' back garden, because Lisa didn't need them all. My mum loves them. They do look pretty good.

"Yes, of course," I reply.

"Actually, maybe I should give her a call, thank her properly. Unless you're going round there soon? You used to be round there every night."

"Um, I'm not sure. Maybe you should call her."

"Are you and Natalie going swimming at the weekend? We're going to have to get you a new swimming costume soon, you just keep growing."

"Um, no, Natalie is having a sleepover with another

girl instead," I reply.

"Oh, that's a shame," says my mum absently as she clatters a saucepan about.

My dad has come late to our conversation. "Are you talking about Natalie? How *is* she? I feel like I haven't seen her for ages!"

"You saw her last week when we planted the flowers," I reply.

"Oh, yes. You will remember to thank her mum for those, won't you?" says my dad.

"Yes, Dad," I reply dully.

"And how was your day, Jessica?" my dad continues, possibly feeling he's heard enough about rounders now.

"Um." I pause. I consider telling my dad that every day is a constant battle to overcome my jealousy and not *cause a scene*. Hmm. I consider showing him Natalie's text, and asking him if he thinks that means she feels guilty about sacking me off. In the end, I opt for, "I learned some new French." (We learn French in Year Six at my school. I know, get us.)

My dad says, "*Bon!*" which is the only French word he knows, and my mum serves up our dinner of beans on toast,

11

and advises us all to tuck in.

"But, Mummy, we had beans on toast yesterday," says Ryan, looking a bit disappointed as he picks up his knife and fork.

My mum shoots Ryan a hurt look that seems to fizz with wronged anger. "Ryan, are you the Chancellor of the Exchequer?" she asks him sarcastically.

Ryan looks like he's not sure if he's supposed to laugh or not. I also can't tell which way this is going to go. "No," he replies.

"I see," continues my mum. "So are you a financial whizzkid of any kind?"

Ryan seems to resign himself to being in trouble. "No," he says sadly.

"Right," says my mum, as if this is news to her. "Then I don't think you can possibly imagine the dire straits the economy is in, and why people all over the world are having to tighten their belts. If you only knew the half of the hardship other families are suffering, or the lengths and sacrifices your father and I are going to, just to make sure we can still put food on the table, you'd be very glad of beans on toast!"

"I didn't say I didn't like it," protests Ryan,

probably feeling this speech he roused from my mum is unwarranted. "I do *like* it."

My mum ignores this for now. "The entire nation is being threatened with financial collapse!"

"I'm sorry," says Ryan, possibly not realising that he is not personally responsible for this state of affairs.

"Mum, leave him alone," I say. "He just made an innocent comment about beans. He doesn't even know what you're talking about."

"You're right, love. Sorry, Ryan," says my mum, instantly calm again (even though no one has made her a cup of tea). "Well, just so's you both know, as of now, this family is on an Economy Drive."

CHAPTER 2

So it turns out an "economy drive" just means my mum isn't going to go shopping until we have eaten everything that's in the freezer. Apart from milk. She will still buy milk. (*Honestly*, she's so *dramatic*, I thought something terrible had happened.)

As I ride the bus to school the next day, I wonder if I am the only sane one in my family. They all took it so seriously. Ryan was particularly upset that the gravy train of Kit Kats is temporarily ending, and ending because there's a load of muesli bars at the back of the cupboard that "no one ever eats". Well, duh – they're *muesli bars*.

Plus, there is to be no discussion of pocket money raises. Luckily I am cheap to keep, and never get invited to McDonald's anyway. See, there is an upside to being unpopular. *Oh* God, I do hope Natalie and Amelia didn't have *too* much fun last night without me.

I feel nervous as I enter my form room, 6C, and see them sitting on their desks, chatting. This really is getting ridiculous. I shouldn't feel nervous entering my own form room.

"Good morning!" I say brightly as I go over and sit down. They're *my* desks, too.

"*Oh, hello*," says Amelia disdainfully, like I am a carpet stain.

"Hey, Jess," says Natalie brightly. "Good night last night?"

Well, let's see. My family announced we're poor while you stuffed your face with ice cream. "Yeah, it was all right," I say vaguely.

"What did you get up to?" asks Natalie.

"Oh, this and that," I say. Mainly playing video games with my six-year-old brother. (You know, I'm keeping it real.)

"By the way, Jess, before I forget, my dad Sky-plussed this ace-looking programme on dinosaurs last night." (Natalie and I are really into dinosaurs at the moment.) "It looks really good. I haven't watched it yet. I was thinking you should come round, and we could watch it together one night."

"Oh my God, I'd love to!" I say. "Hey, and when we watch it, we could eat *dinosaur biscuits*!"

"*Yeah!*" cries Natalie, enthused. "Or, even better – let's *make* them! Let's bake dinosaur biscuits and then eat them and watch the dinosaur programme."

"Yes. This is a brilliant plan," I proclaim. "I can't wait." Natalie grins.

"*Anyway*," sighs Amelia, as if this has all just been some terrible interruption of something amazing she's been saying. "How funny was that last night, when Joe put ice cream in his Coke?"

"Oh, I know!" cries Natalie. They both giggle, remembering.

What the what? They were supposed to be having some stupid deep and meaningful conversation last night in McDonald's. That's the reason they said I couldn't come. Was that a *lie*? Did they fob me off so they could meet boys without me?

"Hey, how come you met Joe?" I ask. "I thought you said—"

"Oh, Joe is such a laugh," Natalie interrupts. "He and Daniel are hilarious."

So *Daniel* was there, too? Why not just invite half the basketball team to McDonald's? What is this conspiracy to exclude me from fun, and ice cream and Coke being mixed hilariously together?

"Yeah, they're so fun," agrees Amelia fondly.

Stop saying it was fun!

You know what? Actually I doubt it *was* that much fun. I mean, sure, Joe and Daniel are good at playing sports for the school, and sometimes do say funny things in lessons, but they're not *that* great. And I happen to think Daniel has quite stupid hair, so there.

"So you met up with Joe and Daniel in McDonald's?" I venture.

"Yeah, it was hilarious, you should have come, Jess," says Natalie, as if she has absolutely no memory of the previous night's conversation.

"You told me not to, remember?" I reply shortly.

"Did I? Oh yeah! Oh, that's right. Yeah. Amelia and I had stuff to talk about, but then we randomly bumped into the boys, and Amelia and I had finished talking by then, so we told them they could join us if they wanted. I was going to text you to come back, but I figured you'd be home by then. It's a shame you weren't there, though. You'd have loved it."

Oh yes. What a shame. What a *sham*, more like! Is this true? It sounds plausible. I can never tell if I am overreacting any more.

"Oh, it was so much fun!" Amelia sighs happily. "Natalie, that's what it used to be like at my old school *all the time*, babes," she explains. (*Babes?*) "There was a group of us that always hung out. A mix of boys and girls. I was kind of like the leader."

(Oh yeah, right, she was the *leader*. There just happens to be no proof for us to check. Oh *yeah*, I'm the most *popular* girl in the school "*back home*".)

"I always made sure we had a really good time," continues Amelia. "I was kind of like, totally this party planner."

"That's so cool," gushes Natalie.

No it isn't, I think. Shut up, Natalie.

"Yeah," says Amelia, agreeing with how cool

18

WACK!

she is. "It was a lot easier there. Everyone was into fashion and stuff. People at this school seem a bit immature." She glances at me. "This school is kind of wack."

"Yeah, this school is totally wack, babes," says Natalie, laughing. (Oh no, don't tell me people are actually *copying* Amelia now.) "Last night was loads of fun."

Why do they have to keep going on about how much fun it was? Well, I'm fun, too! Do they think I'm not fun? Is that it? I could mix ice cream and Coke together if that's the done thing now. (I mean, I could if I can convince my mum to buy either of those two luxury items ever again.) Oh no, they think I'm not fun! I have to show them I'm fun!

Amelia looks quite satisfied with herself, and decides to start a new topic of conversation. "So, Natalie, we need to decide which films we want for the sleepover—"

"I'm having a sleepover," I blurt out.

"*What?*" says Amelia.

"*Are* you?" Natalie sounds impressed.

"Um, yeah, well, I was thinking of having one. I'm not sure yet."

"So you're *not* having one," says Amelia. "Honestly, sometimes I think you're such a—"

Amelia stops dead before finishing whatever insult she had lined up as Tanya Harris has just entered the room.

I'll level with you. I'm a little bit scared of Tanya Harris, but she is kind of my friend.

Tanya Harris is *really* naughty. She once spat in Mrs Cole's face (she got suspended for it) and she put chewing gum in Amelia's hair. I'm fairly certain Amelia is a little bit scared of Tanya Harris too, and I'm pretty sure that's why she's chosen not to insult me in front of her.

"All right, Toons!" shouts Tanya, waving at me from across the room.

"Yep!" I wave back, feeling conscious that this display of greeting is way louder and more attention-seeking than it really needs to be. But that's Tanya.

"Respect. Laters!" she shouts and leaves the room again. Well, that was short and sweet. And loud.

"Honestly, I don't know what's wrong with that girl," mutters Amelia, but very quietly. "She's like,

20

totally weird. And why does she have a nickname for *you*?"

"She likes my cartoons," I reply.

Over the years, I have managed to avoid the worst of the bullying at Hillfern Junior School with my awesome cartooning. That's what I want to be when I'm older, a cartoonist like my hero, Matt Groening. He invented *The Simpsons*. And *Futurama*. And he draws comic strips of rabbits, and my mum let me get a book of one of them,

even though it has the word "hell" in the title.

I don't mean to boast, but I have always been really good at drawing. I love it at school when we get given a work project to do, like, say, "Egypt". I love sketching out all the mummies and sphinxes; I spend ages drawing them. Though then I sometimes run out of time to do any of the writing. And then

I tend to get quite low marks. But I don't care.

I *love* drawing. I can draw a Mickey Mouse and a Homer Simpson that look professional. I draw them all over my books and folders. That's how I have managed to avoid being bullied. People saw them, and asked me to draw them on their books. There were a couple of break times where I had queues!

Then, as we didn't get to choose who we sat next to at the start of this year, I had to sit next to Tanya Harris. I was very worried about this at the time.

One English lesson, Tanya said to me, "Oi, cartoon girl, draw *me* as a cartoon," and passed me her rough book. At first I was terrified. I thought, if I draw her wrong and she doesn't like it, she is going to beat me up at lunchtime. Then I thought, if I don't do it at all, she is still going to beat me up at lunchtime.

But I didn't know what kind of cartoon she would be. All I really knew about her was that she kept being told off for wearing jewellery, and she sometimes hit people. And I didn't think putting that in a cartoon would be the best plan.

But as I thought about it, I remembered she always ate a Cadbury's Creme Egg at break times, so I drew her as a Cadbury's Creme Egg, with arms and legs.

Underneath it I wrote, "Tanya Harris, that's you that is." I passed back her book and waited with bated breath.

She didn't respond until the end of the lesson, then she thumped me on the back and said, "That … is … blimmin' … brilliant!" She loved it. She made me draw another one on a piece of paper, so that she could stick it up inside her desk. She even went over the first one in pen – I'd only done it in pencil – so it wouldn't fade.

But the best part was she showed it to all her friends, who – how can I put this? – happened to be sort of the naughtier boys in our year. Well, they happened to be the very same people who sometimes shouted, "Oooh, chess club" at me, and they all stopped doing it.

So drawing cartoons is sort of my party trick. Like how Linda in our form can turn her eyelids inside out. That's kind of gross actually, I prefer mine.

"Oh, *that*," says Amelia dismissively.

"Yep. Cartoons are my secret superpower," I joke.

"Well, it's lucky you *can* do that," observes Amelia. "Because you certainly can't dress yourself."

SECRET SUPERPOWER

24

CHAPTER 3

There's nothing like a really fun lesson to start the day. And maths is *nothing* like a really fun lesson. Ha ha, I am funny.

I really don't like maths, though. I am extremely sick of long division. It takes too long and all phones have calculators these days. Why don't they just teach us the stuff that technology *can't* do?

Anyway, I sit next to Cherry in this lesson. Natalie and Amelia sit diagonally behind me in the back corner. Like I said, at the start of this year we didn't get to choose who we sat next to because apparently we will choose our friends and then talk during lessons. (Well, obviously, but still.)

I ended up next to Tanya Harris, but she got

25

moved recently because the teachers thought she was looking out the window too much. *Honestly*, our school is *obsessed* with where we sit. It's probably quite unhealthy.

Natalie was chosen to sit next to Amelia, and I suppose because Amelia was new, the teachers couldn't have known they would hit it off so well and whisper more during every lesson than the rest of the class put together. Really, the teachers should admit their plan backfired and let me sit next to Natalie again instead. I mean, they had no problem moving Tanya Harris.

Actually, I don't care anyway. I like sitting next to Cherry. Cherry is in the chess club with me. She's quiet and shy, but very down to earth. (Amelia sometimes calls Cherry fat behind her back, but Cherry always says she feels sorry for "stick insect idiots".) Also, Cherry is clever, and tends to beat Amelia in tests and stuff. So that might be why Amelia is sometimes mean about her. Actually, come to think of it, Cherry tends to beat Natalie in tests and stuff, too. I sometimes think I'm getting bad vibes from Natalie towards Cherry and the rest of the chess club. I wonder if that's why.

We have to sit in the same seats each term for all our lessons apart from the ones in different places like art and PE (obviously). I've totally had to branch out when we go in twos for stuff. In fact, I sort of have more friends now than before Amelia joined our school. I actually know way more people than Natalie and Amelia because they only hang out with each other and a couple of other snooty girls. (Oh yes, and apparently, now *Joe* and *Daniel*.)

"Right, everyone, you should all have a piece of paper on your desk," says Mrs Cole, returning to the front of the room. "The test begins ... now. There will be no talking."

Honestly, a *test. First thing* on a Thursday morning. It's inhumane. If we didn't have art next, I would be feeling a little bit annoyed right now.

There is a muffled giggling noise coming from Natalie and Amelia's corner of the room. I glance over and they are shoving each other, trying not to laugh. Mrs Cole is still at the front of the room and hasn't noticed anything.

I go back to my maths questions. *Typical.* They

12 × 240 = ?

− ✗

even have fun in a horrible maths test.

The giggling noise gets louder, and there is the sound of a desk moving. Mrs Cole is still oblivious. I look round at their corner again and notice Tanya Harris frowning at them with a look of disgust on her face. Suddenly her hand shoots into the air.

"Excuse me, Miss?" she says.

"Whatever's the problem, Tanya?" asks Mrs Cole.

"I think that Natalie and Amelia are cheating in their maths test, Miss. They keep whispering to each other, and then looking at me and laughing. They should be careful, shouldn't they, Miss? Laughing at people is quite rude, isn't it? They might get into all kinds of trouble for doing that."

Natalie and Amelia go bright red and suddenly stop what they're doing. They look quite scared. It *does* really sound like Tanya has directly threatened them in the middle of a maths lesson, with loads of witnesses. There is a weird tension in the room. Everyone is looking at them. Mrs Cole surveys them icily.

"Well, I certainly hope that no one *is* cheating in my lesson. Get on with your work, please, everyone."

Reluctantly, all heads turn back to the maths test.

Natalie and Amelia don't giggle at all for the rest of the lesson.

As the bell goes and we all file out for break, Tanya grabs me at the classroom door and starts chatting to me about how many answers she thinks she got right. She seems a bit distracted, and I realise that she is actually waiting for Amelia and Natalie to come out so she can give them grief.

Suddenly, she breaks off mid-sentence. "Oh, look who it is. Mr and Mrs Snob." Natalie and Amelia ignore her, red-faced, and try to walk past as if nothing is happening. "Yeah, go on, carry on, that's it," Tanya shouts after them as they head down the crowded corridor. "Keep going, and *don't laugh at me again in maths*!"

"Hey, Tanya, go easy," I say. "Natalie's my best friend."

"Is she?" Tanya looks momentarily perplexed. "What about that new one? Amelia Snooty-Face the Third? Well, I can't stand her. Honestly. You know what she thinks, don't you?"

"What?"

Tanya then tells me what she thinks Amelia thinks.

29

I won't repeat it here, but it's along the lines of that her *poop* don't *pong*.

I can't help but laugh. I don't like Amelia, and she *is* mean, and she gets up my nose a lot, but I suppose she is still new, and it must be hard, and I feel bad when anyone gets picked on. Especially if it looks like I'm joining in. Which I wasn't.

I don't manage to find Natalie or Amelia all break. I hope they're not annoyed with me. I hope they don't think I condone Tanya's behaviour.

Maybe I should text Natalie just in case? What can I even put? The bell goes for the end of break and I panic. I write,

Hope U cool. Still best friends, innit? Love J.

I mean, it's a bit soppy, now I think about it. And possibly a bit needy. Hmm. Sometimes I think it would be good if there was a "reverse text" button on phones. Someone should invent that. I— Ooh, Natalie has texted back!

Course we R. Best friends 4eva! UR imagining anything else U nutter. X

30

Phew, art. We're drawing leaves today. I prefer drawing *people* to inanimate objects. I'm not that bothered about leaves, to be honest. I could take them or *leave* them. Ha ha. I am on *fire* today.

I sit next to Joshua in this lesson. Joshua is funny and tall. He's kind of handsome, and really good at basketball. See, I told you I've branched out and made all kinds of friends. Although, I'm not sure I can call Joshua my *friend* exactly.

Once, at the start of this term ('cause there's like six of us all sitting on this one table) I thought a good icebreaker would be to play the "would you rather" game, so I asked him, "Would you rather live for a year in a greenhouse or an igloo?" And he just looked at me like I was mad and said, "Neither."

But the game took off because the others (Terry, Emily, Megan and Fatimah) really liked it, so by the time Terry asked Joshua if he would rather have no teeth or no hair, Joshua was all over it and said he would rather be bald, but I didn't have the guts to ask him any more questions in case he looked at me like I was mad again.

But he might like my leaves joke. I pause with indecision. Then my mouth gets carried away without my consent. "Hey, Joshua?" I say.

"Yeah?"

"I'm not that bothered about drawing these leaves. I could take them or *leave* them!"

"Great, good one," says Joshua sarcastically.

Terry overhears, though, and says much louder, "Hey, I'm not bothered about drawing leaves! I could take them or leave them!" There is a small ripple of laughter around Terry, and people from other tables turn to look at him. (Terry is a joke thief! The cheek.)

"Less noise, thank you, Terry," says Mrs Cooper, our art teacher, coming over. "You don't *have* to draw them, you can always go and stand in the corridor, or outside my office."

Terry doesn't apologise. He just grins broadly, pleased with the level of attention he's receiving. Emily and Fatimah start telling him he is "well cheeky", but this just makes him look even happier.

"Well, Terry liked it," I say drily to Joshua.

Joshua looks at me and smiles. "I think you should

stick to cartoons," he says. Blimmin' cheek! I think. Honestly, Joshua thinks he's *so cool*.

"Does that mean you like my cartoons?" I ask. He looks at me evenly for a moment.

"It means I could take or *leave* your jokes," he replies.

Then he tries to go back to drawing, but stubs his pencil, which breaks, so he ends up with a big line across his page. Ha! I think secretly. Not so cool *now*, are you? Anyway, why do I care?

And honestly, for a joke that's so rubbish, it's been stolen quite a lot within two minutes, I think to myself.

"Oi, Jessica," says Emily. "I done that game on my stepdad. I said, 'Would you rather eat a bowl of live spiders or nothing for three days?' And he said the spiders! I always told my mum he was weird."

The girls on my art table really make me laugh. Emily is more outgoing than Megan and Fatimah. She doesn't care what she says, but Megan and Fatimah nearly always agree with her.

They're different from Natalie, as they don't care

about being cool. And they're different from Cherry and my other chess club friends as they don't care about getting the answers right all the time. In fact, Emily doesn't care at all if she gets stuff wrong. She just laughs it off and carries on.

I laugh. I can feel myself relaxing as I draw my leaves. Honestly, art is *so* much more fun than maths.

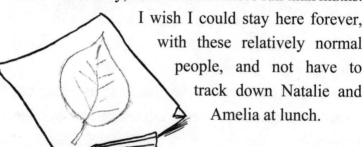

I wish I could stay here forever, with these relatively normal people, and not have to track down Natalie and Amelia at lunch.

CHAPTER 4

Lunch is becoming a pain in the neck, to be honest. I know it's meant to be the highlight of the day, but even without the politics of Natalie and Amelia, it has its problems.

I am (as my mum would put it) in the "wrong wealth-bracket to get the best of it". Basically, we are not poor enough to qualify for free school dinners, but still poor enough that my mum can't give me enough money to get the "nice" food. I can afford coleslaw and a jacket potato, but not lasagne. (Though as my mum has pointed out, I am very lucky to be at a school that *serves* lasagne, even if I can't afford to actually *eat* it.)

I might end up being packed lunch soon anyway.

Depending on how the family economy drive goes. I hope it goes well. I would still rather eat jacket potatoes than muesli bars.

I look everywhere for Natalie and Amelia, but there's still no sign of them. So I end up eating with Cherry and some other members of the chess club. It's quite fun, actually. Cherry tells me about some new brilliant four-move-checkmate thing she has heard of and can't wait to try out. Also, she lets me eat some of her chips.

As I go back into the form room after lunch, I spot Natalie and Amelia. "Hey, there you guys are!" I cry. "Where have you been? I looked everywhere for you!"

"Nothing better to do than look for us? What an exciting life you must lead," says Amelia drily.

I look at Natalie, in case she feels like telling Amelia to be nice like she sometimes does, but she says nothing.

"I was worried you might be annoyed with me or something," I venture, slightly nervously.

"Why would we be annoyed with you?" asks

Amelia.

"I don't know," I say. "It just kind of seemed like you might be avoiding me, or something."

"Avoiding you?" Amelia says, smirking.

"Or something," I repeat.

"No, we weren't avoiding you, Jess, we just had stuff to attend to," says Natalie, and they exchange a look, then smirk.

What is going on? What have they been doing all this time without me? I hope not something awful like snogging Joe and Daniel behind the sports block.

Amelia seems satisfied that I have been wrong-footed and raises her eyebrows at Natalie, as if now they can get back to normal again.

"So, Nat, my dad is going to try and get us tickets to see MBlaze," she says.

Natalie claps her hands. "Oh, I am *so* excited!" she squeals.

Wait a minute. Wait just a cotton-picking minute here. Natalie and I *hate* MBlaze! They're this boy band that we have always agreed are really lame. They wear identical white shirts and think they're hard, but sing ballads about crying because they're so in love all the time. They make me want to *puke*!

Natalie and I used to joke about them all the time, all through Year Five. We said if all they sing about is crying because of love treating them so badly, maybe they should just try being single for a while, and get some hobbies, and stop blimmin' singing about it all the flippin' time!

But then in Year Six a few of the girls started swapping posters of Ricky, and learning the dance moves, and planning their joint weddings to Ricky and Baz. And Natalie and I agreed that we still thought they were lame but that we wouldn't upset anyone by pointing it out. She can't possibly think they're good now!

"You're not serious!" I cry.

"Why not?" asks Amelia.

"MBlaze are so lame!" I say.

"Oh dear, you're *so* immature," sighs Amelia.

"Come off it, Nat, you don't actually *like* them now, do you?"

"Well, I think their last one was quite catchy," says Natalie.

"It wasn't," I assert. "And they're *still* going on about being broken-hearted. Remember how we

38

used to say that was rubbish? Remember when we said they should just get some hobbies?"

"Look, Jessica, people change. And I like them now," says Natalie defiantly.

"Not everyone keeps the same views they had when they were nine," says Amelia unhelpfully.

"Look, just because I don't like some stupid boy band doesn't mean I'm immature!" I say. I can feel my temperature rising. I wonder if I'm blushing. I feel quite hot.

"Whatever," says Amelia. "Look, why don't you just let Natalie get on with her life, stop telling her what she should and shouldn't like, and leave us alone?" She waves one hand at me dismissively. "Go on, run along now."

"Don't you dare speak to me like that, Amelia!" I'm almost shouting now. "You are such an *idiot*!"

"Jess! Don't speak to Amelia like that!" says Natalie. (What about the way Amelia is speaking to *me*? Why is that fine?)

"What?" I say, confused.

"Do you know what, you *are* immature," says Natalie then. "Amelia is right about you." (No she isn't!) "I'm *glad* you're not in our *secret gang*!"

Natalie immediately claps her hands over her mouth, like she didn't mean to say that. Amelia slowly looks at her. I feel strangely deflated, like all the wind has left my sails.

"You're in a … gang?" I ask quietly.

"*Secret* gang," corrects Amelia. "And you're not joining it."

"I don't *want* to join it!" I lie. "Honestly, and you say *I'm* immature. What's it even called? *The Pink Ladies?*" I try to sound scornful.

"God, no. That is *so done*," says Amelia.

"It's called CAC, if you must know," says Natalie. "It stands for Cool Awesome Chicks."

COOL AWESOME CHICKS

"That's cack," I say.

"What?" says Amelia.

"The initials of your gang spell out cac, which sounds like cack. Doesn't that bother you?"

"You don't say it cac, you say the letters CAC," asserts Natalie.

CAC

"No one asked your opinion, actually," says Amelia.

"How long have you been in this gang?" I ask Natalie quietly, feeling almost shy again.

"Well, we've been thinking about it for ages, but we made it official today," she replies.

I feel like I've been dumped, and Natalie and Amelia have just announced their engagement. Which I suppose is kind of what's happened.

I feel a bit like I've been on the verge of being dumped for ages. In some ways this is better. *Oh*, this is so not better. I feel sick. I honestly can't work out if I feel more hurt or angry. Maybe this is the feeling my mum is describing when she says, "This is the *living end*!"

Well, you know what, I can be dignified in defeat. Probably. "Well, thanks for giving me the full picture," I say. "I will leave you two to it." I get up to go.

"Oh, don't be like that, Jessica, we're still best friends," says Natalie.

No, *this* is the *living end*!

"We can't exactly be best friends if I'm not even allowed in your stupid gang," I retort.

"Yes, we can, we just have different interests. I don't complain about you being in the chess club." (Actually, Natalie *has* complained about that. She said it was really annoying that she could never hang out with me on Wednesdays.)

"That's completely different!" I cry. "You could join the chess club at any moment if you wanted. You are deliberately excluding me from your gang."

"Why," says Natalie, "would I want to hang out with a bunch of chess club know-it-alls?"

Amelia laughs. "Actually, how come they let you into that? You don't know anything."

I ignore Amelia for now and plough on. "Look. I would never deliberately exclude you from anything I was doing. That's mean. You're supposed to be my best friend. You said we were best friends forever."

"Oh, boo hoo," says Amelia.

Best Friends forever

"Boo hoo yourself," I snap. "I don't need this." (I'm not sure why I said that.) "Have a nice life," I add sarcastically, and then I walk out of the room.

Dignified in defeat. Oh yeah.

42

As soon as I'm out of the room I run straight to a toilet and lock myself in a cubicle.

Oh *dear*. What am I going to do now? Seriously. What am I going to do? I could stay here in the toilets and cry, I suppose; that's always an option. But that will only take me up to one fifteen, and then I've still got history.

What am I going to do? This really is the *living end*.

CHAPTER 5

So. I did come out of the toilet, fact fans. I stayed in there for about ten minutes, trying to gather my thoughts. My thoughts were quite unhelpful as it happens. They kept veering from a desire to cry, to a desire to smash things.

They've started a gang without me. They've started a *gang* without me. I just couldn't believe it. I still can't believe it. I'm on the bus home now and that sentence is just kind of playing on a loop in my head.

The afternoon flew by. I can't remember anything that happened. I wasn't really paying attention. Now I'm sitting here on the bus, feeling numb about the whole thing. But still kind of angry.

I feel belligerent. I think I want

revenge. Perhaps I should just exclude *them*? But I don't see how not hanging out with them gets me anywhere. That's what they want anyway. I'd just be playing into their hands.

What on earth is the universe playing at? Doesn't it know who I am? I am awesome. I don't deserve this kind of shabby treatment. Do you hear me, universe? *I don't deserve this kind of shabby treatment*. I am a nice person. I deserve to eat lasagne for lunch and not muesli bars, and to have a best friend who actually *likes* me. *Ohhh. Life sucks*.

I arrive home to see my mum in the front garden, chatting to the VanDerks over the little hedge. As I get closer I see she has a slightly pained expression on her face, and is doing her fake smile.

"Hello there, young Jessica," says Mr VanDerk brightly as I approach. "Just been telling your mum here about seeing your sister in the paper."

"Hi, darling. Just the *local* paper," my mum adds dismissively.

(My older sister, Tammy, has left home already.

We don't see her very much. Tammy and my parents don't get on.)

"What's she done?" I ask.

"Tied herself to a tree!" exclaims Mrs VanDerk, and then shrieks with laughter. Mr VanDerk allows himself a little chortle as well.

"She was involved in an environmental protest of some kind," explains my mum.

"Crazy behaviour!" remarks Mr VanDerk. "Are you sure you didn't drop that one on her head when she was little?" Both the neighbours giggle.

My mum does her fake laugh and then says, "No, on the contrary, we brought her up to fight for what she believes in. We're delighted she's doing so well at it."

The VanDerks exchange looks. "Oh yes, of course," says Mrs VanDerk.

My mum presses home her advantage, "I mean, *obviously* I'd *worry* about her less if she was an accountant, but someone's got to save the planet. And anyway," (she injects a jokey air into her voice and puts her arm around me proudly, ruffling up my hair) "*this* one's normal. How was school today, Jessica?"

"It *sucked*," I reply.

My mum's smile falters. I've ruined her grand victory against the oppressive, regime-loving, planet-hating VanDerks. She plays it cool, but her voice goes a bit high. "That's one of the words we don't like you *using,* isn't it, Jessica? Do you remember when we talked about that?"

"I'm *sorry*," I say. Unravelling myself from Mum's arm, I storm inside the house.

Oops. I didn't quite mean to do that. I'm not myself at the moment. I overhear a couple of smug platitudes from the VanDerks about how parenting is so much more complicated these days. I hope my mum's not annoyed with me.

My mum is quite annoyed with me. She came inside and started demanding to know who I thought I was. Apparently "Jessica" was not the answer she was looking for. I tried telling her I'd had a bad day, but she replied it was only going to get worse if I didn't learn to control my temper. My dad had to smooth things over with a cup of tea.

Now it's dinnertime and my dad is still in full smoothness mode. "Ah, this is nice," he says, picking up his knife and fork. *Nooo! Don't say it, Dad!* "Nice family dinner." Oh no, my dad has said the words of doom.

Every time, and I mean *every time,* any meal starts with my dad saying those words it's guaranteed to end with either my little brother or me (usually him) being sent upstairs for messing about. It's like a curse or something. How can my dad not have realised this? How can he not be aware he has just tempted Fate? Again.

And it's not like we started in the best place anyway. My mum is still shooting me dirty looks, and the food is kind of weird. Ostensibly it's roast beef, which obviously should be a massive treat at this stage of the economy drive, but the beef is an old piece of meat Mum found abandoned in the freezer. I'm sure it's safe to eat, but it's kind of dry and chewy, while the "vegetables" are corn on the cob (again, from the freezer). And then the rest of it is instant mashed potato you add hot water to, and gravy. The gravy is delicious. It's Bisto, and it hasn't been frozen or anything.

"Stop pulling faces when you eat that, Jessica," says my mum, as I concentrate possibly too hard on chewing the beef.

"I can't help it," I reply.

"Well, you'd better start helping it," replies my mum.

"This is a violation of my inalienable rights as a citizen," I proclaim.

"Where on earth did you hear that?" My mum looks dumbfounded.

"Eddie Izzard," I say with a shrug. (My dad has some Eddie Izzard stand-up comedy DVDs that I sometimes watch with him.)

"You learned the word inalienable from Eddie Izzard?" says my mum.

"Yeah, he's—"

Mum cuts me off. "Why aren't you getting *much* better marks in English?"

"Because I can't spell," I reply truthfully.

My mum tuts and starts muttering to herself. I can't believe she's still so annoyed with me. She got over Ryan and his abandoned toys much quicker than me just saying "sucked" in front of the VanDerks. And *I* didn't even make her fall over.

Finally we get to the end of the meal. (Ryan has said, "Don't violate my inalienable rights," twice when he's been told not to play with his food, which has made my mum glare at me.)

My dad starts gathering up the plates. I decide to make a joke slightly mimicking him; I reckon it's the only way to lighten the sour mood. So I say, "Ah, there's nothing like a nice roast dinner. And that was *nothing* like a nice roast dinner!" I laugh. Ryan giggles.

My mum says, "That's it! I have had just about enough of you! Get to your room!"

"It was just a joke," I say. "I thought you'd laugh."

"I'm not laughing. Room. Now! This really is the *living end*!"

I quickly scramble out of the kitchen and up to my room. What did I tell you about my dad's doomed sentence? It's all *his* fault, if you think about it.

This is an outrage, I think, as I sit gloomily in my room, staring idly at my dinosaur books. This is all so unfair. I *hate* Natalie and Amelia. I *hate* my mum. All right, I probably don't hate any of them. Maybe Amelia.

It's so unfair that I have been treated like this. It's not right. I want revenge. I have to make a stand. I have to show it's not OK to do this to me. I am a person. I have arguably inalienable rights … I feel all fired up for a second, then I sigh, and feel deflated again, as I have no idea what I can do about any of it.

My bedroom door quietly opens, and Ryan's Lego pirate ship is pushed in, followed closely by a crawling Ryan. He pushes it forwards, as if it is sailing towards me. (My carpet is blue, so it's kind of realistic.) He arrives nearly at my feet, and looks up at me. "Pirates?" he says. He says it in the same matter-of-fact manner as when my Uncle Bob shrugs and says "Pub?" to my dad.

Honestly, *kids*. As if I have time to play Lego pirates. I've got all kinds of wallowing to do. Hmm. Maybe we could have a quick game …

"All right, just for a bit," I say. Ryan jumps up excitedly and goes off to get his Lego pirate base camp. (To be honest, if my parents really wanted to go on an economy drive, they should go back in time and not buy Ryan so many toys.)

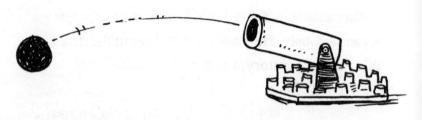

Soon we have it all set up in my room, and Ryan is explaining when he is going to fire the cannon, and how I have to react. It's quite cute how serious he is about all this.

My little brother really looks up to me. I think he is one of the few people who realises that I am awesome. Also, I am a very nice big sister, and I help him with his Lego. I say *help*, I don't want to say *play*, as now I'm in Year Six I'm probably not meant to still play with Lego. I wouldn't tell Natalie, for example … *Oh, what the heck*. I like it. I like Lego pirates. There, I said it. It's really fun.

"… And that's when Jimmy comes out of here to ambush them," Ryan is saying, pointing at a little Lego man with a stripy top and a red bandana. I wasn't completely paying attention.

"Hang on," I say. "I thought Jimmy was the first mate? Why is he going to ambush Captain Blackbeard?"

"Because they fell out over some money," explains Ryan seriously. He's thought a lot about the detail of this pirate backstory, I realise.

"When?" I ask.

"When they stole that gold. Jimmy didn't think he got a big enough share of it, so he formed a rival gang of pirates, and—"

"Wait, hang on, what did you say?"

"Jimmy didn't think he got enough gold, so he formed a rival gang of pirates, and—"

"Ryan, you genius!" I exclaim. Impulsively I grab him and kiss his forehead. *A rival gang of pirates!*

"Urgh!" He shoves me away and scrubs furiously at his damp forehead. "Why am I a genius?"

"You're just, um, you're very good at coming up

with clever pirate stories," I say.

"I *am,* actually," says Ryan proudly. And goes back to spacing out the Lego pirate men for the battle.

CHAPTER 6

I am brilliant. This could work. This could definitely work. I could form a *rival gang* to Natalie and Amelia's stupid load of cac. Ha! That would show them! I'll form a rival gang, and then they won't be allowed to join it! I bet they wouldn't like that at all! It's simple but fiendishly clever.

The more I think about it, the more it seems like a brilliant idea. Oh yes, I would *like* to see that. I would like to see their faces when they get that little piece of news. *How do you like* that, *Natalie and Amelia? Oh look, you don't. Funny that, isn't it?*

Yes! I'm *doing* this! I'm going to do it. I'm so lucky my little brother is into pirate stories. And that I still play pirate Lego with him. See? There is actually a practical application for pirate Lego in the *real* world. (The same cannot be said of long division.)

Just *wait* till Natalie and Amelia see me in my rival gang! Ha ha! *I don't need you any more! I don't need you!* (I won't actually say that out loud – I won't have to.) They will *rue* the day they ever crossed me! (Captain Blackbeard did a lot of rue-ing tonight on my carpet, and believe me, it is not pretty.)

OK. So you probably shouldn't just start a gang out of nowhere, without thinking about it, or giving it a name. That would be ludicrous. I'm not going to be a reactionary idiot about this. I'm going to think about it for at least five minutes, and come up with a really good name and stuff.

OK. I've got it. My gang's name is ACE. It stands for "Awesome Cool Enterprises".

I'm not going to lie to you, it's probably not the best gang name in the world. But you should know, I rejected literally seven other names before I reached it, including "Hilarious Awesome Gang" (HAG) and "Fully Outrageous Organised Lunatics Society" (FOOLS), so it's actually a real winner. And, on the plus side, not only is ACE a better acronym than CAC, but it means we sound like we're probably really ace … *Hmm.* Anyway.

This is going to be brilliant. I feel flushed with excitement as I step off the bus and arrive at school on Friday morning. OK, first I need to get through registration with stupid Amelia and Natalie, and then I can start recruiting people to my gang.

For a moment I'm nervous as I enter 6C, and they are sitting together at our desks, but it all goes eerily smoothly. We just ignore each other. Simple as. I mean, *weird*, obviously. But simple. They don't even whisper to each other about me, or giggle. There's just silence. It's kind of uncomfortable, but I guess it could be worse.

I'm not sure what the best approach to recruiting people for a gang is. The only people I know who are in one are Natalie and Amelia, and I can hardly ask them how they did it. I figure I'll just ask everyone I know if they want to join, and see who's up for it.

I sit next to Cherry in most of my lessons. Double geography first thing on Friday morning is no exception. I decide to ask her and Shantair (who sits on the other side of Cherry and is also in the chess club). They seem as good a place to start as any.

But to be honest, when I broach the subject (while we are supposed to be quietly shading in maps of Europe) they don't seem bowled over by the idea. If anything, they seem a little bit suspicious of it.

I mean, I suppose it doesn't help that Shantair and Cherry are really hard-working and love trying their hardest at everything, so they think I'm interrupting their learning. (That's probably one of the few downsides of my chess club friends – they don't approve of whispering in lessons.) Natalie and Emily and the others positively love whispering when we are meant to be learning.

"But why?" asks Shantair. "What would we do in the gang?"

"Just hang out and stuff," I answer. "But we'll know we're in a secret gang." (I don't really know anything about what you're actually *meant* to do in a gang. Maybe I should google it?) "Kind of like being in the chess club," I add with an inspired flourish.

"But we're already in the chess club," says Cherry, sounding confused.

"I know. So it will be slightly different. But, you know … um, *look*, do you want to join or not?" I'm starting to feel a bit cross. People should *want* to join, surely? I mean, I'd want to join a secret gang if someone asked me. Am I the only one that thinks it sounds exciting?

"Would I have to do anything?" asks Cherry.

"No, you wouldn't have to do anything," I say.

"All right, fine," says Cherry.

"Yeah, fine," agrees Shantair.

"Great!" I say. "We're called ACE – and remember, it's a secret." *We can work on your negative attitudes*

later, I add silently.

I start to perk up again at break time. Who cares if they're reluctant? They've still joined. They'll see it's fun once we get going. I have two members already! This is still going to be brilliant.

I bump into Tanya Harris in the corridor near our form room. I wonder if I should invite Tanya to join? I mean, she probably won't want to, but I did say I'd ask everyone I knew.

"All right, Toons?" she says. "What's new with you?"

"Actually, Tanya, I've just formed a gang," I say proudly.

Tanya gives a little chuckle and then looks at me quizzically. "What?" she says.

"I've just formed a gang," I repeat.

"*You* have?" She looks quite surprised.

"Yes. We're called ACE. It stands for Awesome Cool Enterprises—"

I don't get much further as I'm distracted by how much Tanya is laughing. She has to lean against the wall and when she stands up straight again, her

60

face is red and she has to wipe tears away from the corners of her eyes.

Once she has finally stopped laughing, all I can get out of her is that she thinks I am "well bare jokes", which (I'm not going to lie to you) I think might mean she's not a hundred per cent sold on the idea of ACE.

I decide to plough on anyway. "Do you want to join my gang?" I ask.

Tanya splutters more laughter. "Stop it, stop it," she says. "My stomach hurts."

"I don't see why it's *that* funny," I say.

"The thing is with gangs, Toons, is they're not normally called things that go on about how nice and awesome they are. Haven't you ever heard of the Crips and the Bloods?"

I have *heard* of them, but I don't know exactly what they are. I think they were rival gangs in Los Angeles, with guns or something.

"Well, yes, OK. But this is going to be a nice gang. Theoretically, you could have a nice gang, couldn't you?"

Tanya looks at me seriously for a moment. I get the distinct impression that, despite laughing in my face, she doesn't actually want to offend me.

"Maybe *you* could," she says. "But Tanya Harris can't go joining no nice gang. I've got my reputation to think of. I'm a lone wolf. Don't fence me in. No one can put a label on Tanya 'the Beef' Harris."

"Tanya 'the Beef' Harris?" I repeat.

"It's just a nickname I'm trying out. I'm hoping it will catch on. Pass it on."

"Uh, sure."

"Tell you what," she says. "I'll be your muscle, if you need it, for your gang. But just freelance. If anything kicks off, I got your back."

I didn't understand any of that. "Um, OK, thanks, Tanya. That's brilliant."

OK, so. On the one hand, I have been quite seriously laughed at and no one *really* wants to join my gang. But, on the other hand, it's technically going well in that I have 2.5 members already. (Depending on what Tanya actually meant.)

I try to jolly myself along. I just have to be positive. I mean, this is really just a glass half-empty/half-full situation. Or maybe it's more a situation where I thought I had this really brilliant glass, full of the most delicious drink ever, but it turns out I'm just holding an empty, value supermarket brand, multi-pack cola can.

No, I should be positive. And it's actually been much easier than I feared to avoid Natalie and Amelia. I don't sit with them in most lessons, and I didn't look for them at break time. Well, I didn't *see* them. I kept half an eye out, but I didn't *actively* look for them. Not like before, anyway.

They weren't in the form room. They were probably off doing something *secret*. Well, wait till they see how secretive *I* can be, when I start parading *my* secret gang in their stupid faces!

Although, then it won't be a secret. Well, I'll have to tell them about the initial secret, so that they *know* there is something they don't know. I'm sure that's how it works.

This thought spurs me on to be even more positive. Plus, now it's French and French is in the exciting new building. Our school got a grant or something to start teaching languages. Though I don't see why we needed a whole new classroom. The only difference as far as I can see is that we have headphones in this room.

Anyway, in French
I sit with Emily, Fatimah and Megan (the girls from my art table) and they're bound to want to join ACE. Aren't they? I just have to sell it right.

The thing about getting Cherry and Shantair to join was I had to make it sound like an *extracurricular* interest. That way they felt like they were somehow *achieving* something by joining. (They love extracurricular interests: Cherry plays the violin, and Shantair goes to a drama club at the weekends.)

But Emily, Megan and Fatimah seem to hate doing anything that sounds like it might be work, so with them I'm going to have to play up the *fun* element.

We're doing group work in this lesson, where we

64

take it in turns to ask each other what our names are and how many brothers and sisters we have. (In French, obviously. If we had to speak in English, it would be *easy*.)

"Hey, I have to ask you guys something," I say. They look at me, interested.

But then Miss Price, the French teacher, comes over to us and hovers, so I quickly have to revert to "*J'ai un frère et une soeur*" instead.

Miss Price finally leaves us (after a quick discussion with Emily about whether or not the French book is stupid for not including the French for stepdad). And I drop my secret-gang bombshell.

I think I may have overused the word "secret" this time, as I was trying to make it sound more appealing. But these guys seem really interested. They keep grinning at each other, and they all lean in to hear more when Emily asks what *kind* of secret gang it is.

Hmm, maybe I should have googled "gangs" at break time as I'm still not sure I have a satisfactory answer to that question. I switch to being evasive and overusing the word "fun" instead. Maybe I should suggest sleepovers?

"Who else is in the gang?" asks Fatimah.

"Yeah, how many members are there?" asks Megan. "You don't want too many, or it won't be very secret."

"Yes, no, exactly," I say. "Other than me, there are two and a half members so far."

"How are there two and a half members?" asks Emily.

"Well, Cherry and Shantair joined outright, and Tanya Harris said she'd be freelance."

"What does that mean?" asks Emily.

"I don't know," I admit.

"Tanya Harris?" Fatimah sounds slightly in awe.

"I think it's going to be really fun," I say. "We should have sleepovers."

"Yeahhh!" whispers Emily excitedly. "I'm well up for that. Count me in."

The others say "Me too" pretty quickly after that. *Sleepovers*. That's the way forward. Maybe I should buy my mum a present to say sorry for annoying her, and then she might actually let me have one? Hmm.

Anyway, never mind that now. That's a technicality. We have to celebrate! I have successfully formed a gang! There's six of us (not counting Tanya, which something tells me I shouldn't).

I round everybody up at lunch (except Tanya) and insist we all eat together, to mark the occasion. It's the first ever ACE meeting.

Everybody seems a little bemused at first. Shantair and Cherry don't really have that much in common with Emily, Megan and Fatimah.

Shantair and Cherry are fairly shy, quiet and studious. I mean, they technically know Italian, just from learning music. Emily, Megan and Fatimah are louder, and don't care at all about getting good marks. Plus, Megan thought "arpeggio" was a golfer. So at first it's a bit awkward, what with Cherry trying not to laugh in Megan's face.

But after I make us all clink our drinks together, and start talking about how we probably should invent a secret handshake, they all get a lot more enthusiastic. And it turns out they actually have loads in common with each other. (Well, OK, so far they all like chips but it's a start!) This is *brilliant*!

I *knew* this would be brilliant. I should listen to myself more often. I'm brilliant. I knew I was. What was all that worry about glasses being half full and half empty before? The rule is: I'm brilliant. That should just be a rule.

And now the moment I've been waiting for since I came up with this idea.

I enter my form room towards the end of lunch. Natalie and Amelia are sitting on our desks, as usual. I go over to them.

"Oh hello, I didn't see you there," I say casually, sitting down.

"Well, you obviously did see us," says Amelia.

"Speaking to us now, are you?" asks Natalie.

Me? Not speaking to *them*? It takes two people to not speak to each other, and they weren't speaking to me *either*! Not important, I realise. Calm, happy thoughts.

"So, how's it all going with the gang?" I ask, trying to sound earnest.

Natalie and Amelia exchange looks with each other. "Fine, thanks," says Natalie.

"Good, good. They can be so tricky, can't they?" I continue.

"What would you know about it?" asks Amelia.

"Well, it's a very good question that you ask there actually, Amelia. What would *I* know about it? Well, quite a lot, as it happens. As I have just formed my *own* secret gang."

"KERPOW! Take *that*! Yeah! Feel it! I slammed you!" I add (silently in my head), looking eagerly from one to the other. To be fair, they do look surprised and confused, and keep looking at each other and then back at me. This is *brilliant*.

"You?" says Natalie finally.

"Yep," I say.

"You do know you're meant to actually put a bit of thought into stuff like this?" says Amelia, sounding quite annoyed. "You can't just copy people. You need to think about it, and have a name—"

"Got a name, thanks," I interrupt.

"What's your name?" Natalie sounds interested.

"ACE," I say proudly. "It stands for Awesome Cool Enterprises. I think it's a nice message, really. And

of course, the other advantage of ACE as a name is that the acronym doesn't spell out one of the milder swear words for poo."

Zing! I *love* being in a gang. This was all totally worth it. What a difference a day makes. This time yesterday I was in a toilet trying not to cry. And this time today I feel on top of the world, and Natalie and Amelia look really annoyed with me.

"You won't get away with this," says Amelia. But I just don't even care.

CHAPTER 7

Ah, life is good. The last couple of days have really flown by. ACE has been going really well (although we haven't really done much yet) and things just seem calmer generally.

Natalie and Amelia have gone back to not speaking to me. It's a pretty frosty atmosphere with them. They whisper about me, I'm sure, but they don't giggle. They seem kind of angry with me. I don't know why.

Well, I mean, I *do* know why, I know exactly why. But if it's not meant to be that big a deal that they formed a gang – and apparently no cause for me to be upset – then surely it follows that it shouldn't be a big deal if I do it back to them. Which actually, if anything, just goes to prove that they *do* think it's a

big deal and they are lying hypocrites! They have tasted their own medicine and found it bitter! (Also they think I'm a copycat. But I don't care.)

Everything's been calmer at home, too. I bought

my mum a little box of Roses chocolates on my way home from school on Friday, as a kind of a sorry present, and she was delighted. In fact, she said she "would have to send me to my room more often, if this was the result", which was really not the message I was trying to drive home.

My parents keep commenting on how they haven't seen much of Natalie lately, which is annoying. I don't want to have to explain that we aren't friends any more. Plus, they really like Natalie. They might be upset that she's turned evil.

Now it's Monday, and I'm on the bus to school again after quite a relaxing weekend. It feels a bit weird having not seen or spoken to Natalie all this time, I suppose, but in a way, nice not to have been on eggshells, or worrying I'm losing her by not being cool enough.

I'm not sure how long this is going to go on for.

I mean, I guess part of me thought they might go, "OK, point taken" and include me or something. But that hasn't happened. It's a kind of stalemate. No one's really "won". I don't see how that can change. Unless they up the ante.

As I enter my form room I see a bigger group of girls than usual crowded around Natalie and Amelia's desks. There's too many of them for the space, so the overflow has meant they're round my desk too. They are all chattering excitedly, but they suddenly stop as they see me approach and kind of stare at me. One of them is actually sitting *on* my desk.

"Uh, hi," I say. They are all friends of Natalie's and Amelia's. They're from 6P, the other form group.

"*Uh, hi.*"

"*Uh, hi.*"

They appear to be doing impressions of me, and then they start giggling. Oh, *great*. Well, this is *technically* bullying. I feel my face start to get a bit hot.

"Um, you're actually sitting on my desk, actually," I say to the one called Cassy.

"Yeah, so?" she replies. More giggling.

"Well, it's *my* desk." I start to feel annoyed, as

well as hot and bothered. I look her in the face. I look round at all of them. Natalie and Amelia are there in the middle, really enjoying this.

"It's a free country," she says.

And then I spot them. They are all wearing *badges*! They are all wearing really cool pink and purple badges that say "CAC" on them. This is their gang and they all have badges to prove it. God, that's *amazing*, I think reluctantly.

"So is this CAC, then?" I ask.

"Ah, bless. And you said she wasn't that bright," Cassy says sarcastically to Amelia. (How *rude*. I *am* bright! I know the word inalienable.)

"Yeah," says Amelia to me. "I take it you've spotted the badges then."

"Yes, very nice, well done. You must be very pleased," I say, as if I'm a miffed parent who has been forced to congratulate someone else's child on Sports Day.

"Cassy has a badgemaker," says Amelia.

"*I* have a badgemaker," says Cassy.

"I think it's the sort of thing you need to do, really," says Amelia. "If you want to be a *proper* gang. Not

74

just some wannabe."

They all look at me expectantly, as if they want some kind of response to this. I don't really have anything to say about it, though.

"Look, just get off my desk!" I say finally. Cassy jumps down. I think I shocked her.

"Bell's probably about to go anyway," she quickly explains. The others all get up, too.

"OK, see you back here at lunch, same meeting place," says Natalie.

Meeting place? No, look, my *desk* cannot become their meeting place. No way. That is so *mean*.

"No," I hear myself say. Cassy and the other CAC members turn back to me. I say to Natalie, "They're not in our form, actually. So, it's probably not the best place, is it?"

Natalie rolls her eyes. "It probably doesn't matter, does it?"

"I think it does, though," I say.

"I don't think it does," says Natalie.

"I think it does, though," I repeat.

"Yeah, but I don't think it does."

"Yeah, but I do think it does," I say again.

The CAC heads are swivelling between Natalie

and me. Amelia eventually interjects. "We'll text you," she says, and they leave.

Oh my goodness. I can't believe that just happened. They have upped the ante all right. They are shoving down my throat exactly how much I am being excluded! They are totally trying to rub in my face that they are a better gang than ACE. It's outrageous. Now, I may not know much about the world, but I do know this: I *need* a badgemaker!

So. What has two thumbs and no badgemaker? *This guy*. (You can't see me, but I am pointing at myself, with my thumbs. Geddit?)

My mum has been *very* unreasonable about the whole badgemaker thing.

"Kids! Dinner!" she calls up the stairs.

I mean, she didn't even *listen* when I told her about how it would be an *investment*. It might even *make* money. I told her I could sell the badges I made to the other students, and everything. She is far too fixated on what is legal, if you ask me.

"Kids! Dinner!" she shouts again.

Reluctantly I follow Ryan downstairs and plop

down at the table.

"There you are," says my dad. "Helmet off, please, Ryan." Ryan woefully removes his space helmet. We all seem to be a bit bleak.

My mum serves us up some lamb burgers that had been in the freezer and some mixed vegetables that had been there too. And the last of the Bisto gravy. To be fair, this is much nicer than that weird roast the other day. If anything, this is one of the nicest meals of the money-saving enterprise. What a shame I am too blue to enjoy it properly.

"So, how was school—" my dad starts, but I interrupt.

"*PLEASE*, can I have a badgemaker?"

"Oh, not this again," snaps my mum. "No, Jessica! I've told you no! No means no!"

"But—"

"No."

"It's less than ten pounds to get one."

"Ten pounds is too much money."

"Yes, but it's *less* than that. So that's good."

"No."

"*Please*. I never ask you for anything." My parents just look at me, so I continue anyway. "Ryan gets everything *he* wants."

"No, I don't," says Ryan, sounding slightly annoyed at being dragged into this.

"No, he doesn't," says my mum. "We treat you exactly the same. And Ryan doesn't have a mobile phone, and we won't have to fork out for an expensive new school uniform for him in six months' time."

"It's not *my* fault I need a new school uniform. And that's ages away, and you said you can get loads of it second hand."

"The answer is no, Jessica. Don't make me send you to your room again." My mum sounds so tired and weary that I drop it.

"OK, fine," I sigh.

But now *my mum* won't drop it. "You seem to have forgotten we are on an economy drive!"

"I know," I say crossly.

"Do you?" says my mum. "Do you really? Do you understand what that means?"

"Yes!" I say, annoyed.

"I'm not sure you do," she says. "You kids don't know the first thing about the meaning of work, or the value of money ..."

Oh *great*, now she's going off on one about work ethics. So she's obviously *completely* forgotten about the time when I volunteered/was coerced by her into helping at that cake sale, to raise money for the old people's home. (I was actually really good at it, and at the end I got given a free cream slice from

one of the old people.) How's that for appreciating the value of work? Exactly.

I suppose that actually my parents are quite hardworking, sensible people. I mean, they are quite taken with the idea of *good* jobs. Tammy says this is because they have a Protestant work ethic, and it's people like them who are largely responsible for the rise and success of capitalism. (Which is one of the reasons they don't get on that well.)

"Mum, I get it, and I *have* dropped it," I point out.

"And a *badgemaker*, anyway?" She's on a roll.

"You've never mentioned one before. Just some fad, is it? You'll use it once and then never again. I expect someone at school has one, do they?"

"*No*," I lie, trying to sound outraged.

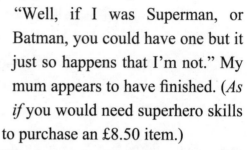

"Well, if I was Superman, or Batman, you could have one but it just so happens that I'm not." My mum appears to have finished. (*As if* you would need superhero skills to purchase an £8.50 item.)

"If you were Batman, you could easily afford one," I retort. "Bruce Wayne is a zillionaire."

"It's a shame you're not a superhero called *bank manager man*," my dad tells me. "And your superpower was *managing the economy*." He chuckles.

"Yes, very funny, Dad," I say tiredly. My dad looks quite pleased with himself.

Frankly, it's a shame I'm not a superhero, full stop. With any super skills. Or just any skills. Although, I *do* have *some* skills. And I sometimes joke that they are my superpowers … Hey, I think I might have just had a brilliant idea!

CHAPTER 8

I can't believe I didn't think of this sooner. I am a *cartoonist*. (At least, that is what I want to be.) I will *make* my own badges. That is, I will draw personalised cartoons of everyone in my gang, and I will stick them on to existing badges that we already have lying around the house. It's genius!

I need seven in total. I quickly round up a few I have lying about my room. One is from a Christmas panto and says "I love Buttons". Another says "I heart Tinkerbell". I find some in a kitchen drawer that say "Meat Is Murder", which I think my sister must have left there. And I get the rest from Ryan who says he doesn't need his Transformers badges any more. I have *way* more than I need. This is brilliant!

Right then. I sit at my desk and set about drawing everyone. It's actually a lot harder than I thought it would be. I really want these to be good. I rack my brains trying to think of the best cartoons of what people could be.

Some are easier than others. For Tanya Harris, I just draw her as a Cadbury's Creme Egg again. I make Shantair a cartoon chess piece castle, as that is her favourite chess piece. She always uses her castles loads. I make Cherry some cherries. I make Emily a dolphin as she really likes dolphins and sometimes gets me to draw them on her books.

I do some rough sketches of each one. Then I decide which is the best version of each of the rough sketches. I make that the official one and draw it neater. Then I copy as carefully as I can the neat version of each cartoon on to some white card. I colour them in with my paints as neatly as I can, deciding I will leave them to dry overnight before I cut them out.

At the bottom of each one, I paint "ACE" in red, with a yellow, zigzaggy, comic book-style explosion thing behind it. I think it looks pretty good.

The whole process takes *hours*. Towards the end my dad starts threatening to turn my light out if I don't go to bed immediately. But finally, *finally* (after a tiny row about how many times I have said "ten more minutes"), I am finished.

Ryan comes in to say goodnight wearing his Buzz Lightyear pyjamas and holding his Winnie the Pooh bear, and admires my handiwork. He seems genuinely impressed. "I want one," he says.

"I've only got enough for my friends at school," I explain.

"Do one for me. I want to be Ryan the cartoon."

"But it's kind of for a gang, Ryan. You're not really—"

His face falls. "*Please*," he says.

"Oh, all right," I say, sighing. "You can be an honorary member. But I'm only doing this once. If you break or lose this, that's it."

Ryan nods enthusiastically. "I'm a spaceman," he says.

"Well, *duh*," I reply. Ryan giggles. (That was a no-brainer.)

"Kids? Ryan? Are you in bed yet?" calls my dad.

"Hang on, Dad!" I call back. "Just ten more minutes!"

OK, it's Tuesday morning and my cartoons are cut out and superglued on to actual badges. I am ready to go. We have lift-off. My mum has banned Ryan from wearing his to school. She says it's against regulations. I have to pointlessly promise her I won't wear mine at school. (Some people's priorities are just all over the place.)

I even told her about how Melissa in our form wears a badge all the time, but she didn't listen. Admittedly, I didn't add that Melissa's badge says "Form Captain".

My badge is of a cartoon paintbrush, Megan is a kitten (she just got one and loves it) and in the end I made Fatimah a Jelly Baby (because she loves them). I'm so excited as I ride the bus to school. I can't wait to give these out to everyone.

And I don't even have to wait that long because we have art first thing on a Tuesday morning.

I try and attract the attention of Emily, Megan and Fatimah, without alerting Joshua or Terry, who I fear may mock my endeavours. (But also because it's a *secret*.)

"Hey, psst." I try and get their attention. "ACE now has badges." I proffer the little Tupperware box the badges are in. "We should wear them for meetings and stuff."

Emily, Megan and Fatimah stare at the box in confusion for a moment, and then as realisation dawns on them they get really excited. "Oh my gosh! These are brilliant!" cries Emily, tipping the whole lot out on to the desk.

"Amazing!" coos Fatimah.

"Which one am I?" asks Megan.

Predictably, all this does get the attention of Terry and Joshua but they don't say anything at first. I dish out the badges and explain the thinking behind them. The gang members put them on, delighted, and seem really pleased.

"This must have taken you *ages*," says Emily.

"It did," I agree.

"Let's see, then," says Terry, and the remaining badges get passed round him and Joshua. They don't "ooh" and "aahh" as much as the girls did, but Terry says, "Very nice." And then passes them back.

"We're in a gang," says Megan, by way of explanation.

"There is rather too much noise coming from this table," says Mrs Cooper, coming over. I quickly scrabble the remaining badges into the box before she sees. We all go quiet. She seems satisfied and goes back to explaining the difference between tints and tones. We pay attention for a bit and start copying what she is showing us.

"I like your cartoons," Joshua says to me quietly.

"Really?" I say, surprised, looking at him curiously. "Thanks." He looks like he might be blushing. Is he? Is he blushing? I think he is!

"They kind of remind me of, well, I suppose you've got kind of a manga style," he says. "Do you like much manga?"

Ha ha! Joshua *is* blushing! He's normally so cool (or at least he thinks he is). I resist the urge to shout "Ha ha! You're blushing!" and try and focus on the conversation.

Hmm. How best to answer this question? OK. I know what manga is. It's a style of Japanese cartoon

86

comics. I don't know if I can truthfully say that I'm *into* it, as such. But I have seen a few of the animated films, now I think about it. And I did especially like that one my sister showed me about the environmental princess warrior.

"Well," I say, "I quite liked *Princess Mononoke*."

"Oh, cool," says Joshua, sounding impressed. "I liked it too."

We shade in tints and tones for a bit. "So, you're in a gang?" he asks quietly.

"Yeah, that's right," I reply. I suddenly feel like I must sound very interesting.

"Like the Crips and the Bloods?" he says jokingly. Is he mocking me again?

OK, maybe I'm not *that* interesting. But, hello? There *are* other gangs. Why does everyone have to keep comparing my gang to the Crips and the Bloods all the time?

Crips and Bloods

"Yes, that is in fact where I got the idea," I joke.

"Yeah, I thought it must be. So who are your rivals?"

"Eh?" (How does he know about that?)

"Who are ACE's turf war rivals?" (Oh, right, he's still joking.)

"Oh. Um. There *is* a rival gang, actually," I say.

"No way!" He laughs.

"Way," I say. And I somehow end up telling him all about Natalie and Amelia having another gang, and how one of their members has a badgemaker, so I had to up my game and pull these cartoons out of the bag.

Joshua listens to everything with interest, but also with an amused expression on his face. I can't tell if he's mocking me. Finally he says, "Wow. Well, I guess you can tell we live in suburbia."

He *is*! He's mocking me again. The nerve. "That's a slightly long word for you, isn't it?" I say. "What do you mean?"

"Ha *ha*," he says sarcastically, blushing slightly. Then he recovers himself. "Most gangs have fights in the inner cities, with knives, you know, urban turf warfare, bloodshed on the streets. You lot are doing a battle with *badgemakers*."

I can't help but laugh, although I also might be going a tiny bit red. It does sound really lame when he says it like that. But like, *hello*? That's not the *point*.

"There's still a principle at stake," I splutter.

Joshua has stopped blushing by now, but suddenly he looks slightly unsure of himself again. "Oh I know, I didn't mean to knock you. Good for you with your principles." (I can't tell if he is being sarcastic or not.) Then suddenly he says, "Hey, I'm reading a GTO manga cartoon book at the moment. I'll bring it in to show you sometime, if you like?"

"Um, yeah, OK, sure," I say, feeling confused. "Sounds good." *Whatever*, I think. I'll believe that when I see it.

Tanya predictably doesn't want to wear her badge, though she tells me she thinks it is "blimmin' brilliant" when she grabs me at lunch and I show it to her. She seems kind of preoccupied with how angry she is at having been given another detention. It sounds like she got it for shouting, but she is insisting to me that she wasn't, and that she has been "stitched up".

"I hate this school," she says. "I hate Hillfern Juniors! *Hell*fern Juniors more like. Can you make that into a cartoon for me, Toons? This place being like hell?"

"Er, yeah, sure," I hear myself say. *Great*. Now I have cartoon homework.

OK. Everyone in ACE who's going to is wearing their badges. I realise that I've been slightly dishonest so far. I haven't told any of them we even *have* rivals, and now it's the end of lunch and I've made them all congregate outside my form room so that we can "practise" our new secret handshake.

I know full well that Natalie and Amelia will be arriving back at the form room any minute and will see us in all our personalised-badge glory. And sure enough, almost on cue, they arrive.

"Oh honestly, this is *tragic*," says Amelia loftily, when she realises what we are doing.

"Who are you calling tragic?" says Emily, annoyed.

"They're just jealous because we're in a better gang than them," I say to Emily.

"Oh, are you in a gang as well?" Fatimah asks

them. Everyone has pretty much stopped doing the secret handshake now.

Amelia gives her a look as if she can't decide if Fatimah's joking or not. "And I suppose you all have *badges* now as well, do you?" she says scathingly. She and Natalie look at us all.

"Yes, we do," says Emily. "Jessica was up half the night making them, and they're brilliant."

"Oh wow, you made them!" Natalie can't quite hide how impressed she is. "Let's see." She peers more closely at some of the badges. "I love the dolphin."

"Well, I don't like any of them," says Amelia, sounding increasingly annoyed.

"Oh, yeah, I don't like them *that* much." Natalie tries to recover herself.

"Well, are we supposed to be *scared* of you, Jessica? Are you going to fight us or something?" says Amelia. "Is that what this is?"

Honestly, what a *hypocrite*! She's perfectly happy to get her gang together to pick on *me*. At my *own* desk. And none of us has even picked on her right now, *she* started on us!

"No, Amelia," I say. "This is hardly the Crips and the Bloods." (OK. I must learn some other gang names.) "But just do be aware that we exist, and you might want to be careful about who you gang up on in the future."

"That sounded like a threat," says Amelia. "Is that what you think you're doing, Jessica? If I *cuss* you will one of your gang *get me back*? Is that what you do? Do you defend each other's honour?"

"I'm not bothered," says Shantair. (Shantair is quite pacifistic, even for a member of the chess club.)

"What?" says Amelia.

"I'm not bothered about that," explains Shantair. "I think that's a stupid reason to start a fight."

Part of me wants to laugh at how wrong-footed Amelia looks. *Nice one, Shantair*, I think.

"Yeah, we're obviously a more peaceful, fun gang than you," I say. "We just want to hang out and have fun and stuff."

"Oh good, well enjoy hanging out then," says Amelia. "We hang out, too. A lot more than you do. Probably in better places."

Amelia seems to be losing her cool. Natalie takes her by the arm and leads her into the form room away from us. She does have one glance back in the direction of the dolphin badge, and then they're gone.

I think that went very well, considering. I mean, admittedly Amelia wants to kill me. But I think Natalie really wishes she had one of my handmade badges. How good is that?

CHAPTER 9

I feel really pleased with myself as I sit at my desk later that night, shading in the picture of my school as hell for Tanya. I've just kind of drawn a building with fire behind it, and "Hell Fern Juniors" in spooky Halloween writing as the sign on the gate. There are people running around screaming a bit as well, but I think it looks kind of cool. Hopefully Tanya will like it anyway.

And luckily, none of ACE have been annoyed with me for not mentioning Amelia and Natalie's gang sooner. They don't seem bothered by her at all. They just think she's overreacting and being silly. I always imagine people must be as intimidated by Amelia as I am, but I'm quite glad they're not.

Of course, she *will* retaliate. And it probably won't be pretty when she does, but for some reason I feel quite buoyed up by the fact that Natalie really seemed to like my badges. Maybe that's a sign that this whole gang thing has gone too far, and no one meant it to get silly, and maybe we'll all be friends again soon?

I mean, I just wanted to make a point. I didn't want to be actual enemy rivals with them. I was kind of hoping they'd go, "Hey, you're a force to be reckoned with, we misjudged you and will never cross you again," or something. You know, like what everyone says is meant to happen when you stand up to bullies – they don't just beat you up even more, no, you earn their respect. Or something. I don't know.

Anyway, the point is, I have made my point. I'm pretty sure I have. I'm feeling quite optimistic about it actually.

When will I learn? Never be optimistic, Jessica. Never. It just makes everything so much harder when you have to adjust back to reality again.

I entered my form room this morning (Wednesday)

and there was no sign of Natalie or Amelia at all. On my desk was a posh, white piece of card, with specially printed pink and silver writing on it.

It said, *"Dear member of CAC. You are hereby invited to the official CAC outing this weekend ..."* Then it listed where they were meeting (the mall) and what they were going to do (the cinema and the pizza place) and even advised on bringing enough money for popcorn and stuff.

As I held it in my hand, for one second I thought that maybe it was for *me*. I mean, they put it on *my* desk. Maybe Natalie and Amelia were really sorry that things had escalated and got daft, and maybe they wanted to include me in their gang after all.

I immediately thought this was unlikely, but for some reason my brain really latched on to it, and played out this whole scenario for me. Natalie had probably had to talk Amelia round a bit. She'd probably said, "Look, Amelia, Jessica is my best friend, and either she's in or I'm out," and Amelia would have had to let her have her way.

I imagined Natalie and Amelia coming back into the form room, and Natalie begging me to be her friend again, and I'd say, "It's OK, of course I forgive you! Don't speak another moment. Let's just be best friends again!" And then we'll hug, and an orchestra will play in the background, and the rest of the form will clap and cheer.

Like I say, I got kind of carried away with the idea. And I was still sort of in this daydream, holding the invite, when Natalie and Amelia *did* come back into the form.

Except Amelia said, "Urgh, you-know-who is touching one of our lovely invites."

And I said, "It's OK! I forg—"

And Amelia said, "What?"

And then I quickly said, "It's OK, I fo-und your invite for you. You left it on my desk." And I handed it back to her.

And now I'm just kind of standing here, looking at them, and really trying not to cry, because I feel so disappointed that my fantasy of Natalie wanting to be my friend again hasn't come true. It's like I've lost her all over again.

"Well, at least you haven't messed it up too much," says Amelia nastily, studying the card.

Anger shoots through me, despite feeling hopelessly near the verge of tears. "Well, you obviously left it on my desk because you wanted me to see it," I say. "I think you need to work on your secrecy skills, Amelia. Not much of a *secret* gang at the moment, is it?"

"All right, calm down," says Amelia, clearly enjoying herself. "No need to get angry about it – unless – you didn't think it was for *you*, did you?" She grins.

I *hate* Amelia. "No, of course not," I lie.

"Just because it was on your desk," adds Amelia.

"Well, why *was* it on my desk?" I ask. "I mean—"

"Aha! So you *did* think it was for you!" She laughs and nudges Natalie. "Aww, that is *so sad*," she giggles. "As if we'd want you along, in your Primarni best."

"I think you wanted me to think it was for me," I say. "I think you're playing nasty tricks."

"Oh, look who's talking!" says Amelia. "At least I can think of my *own* tricks. Instead of copying other people's all the time."

"*Whatever*," I say. "And for the record, I didn't think it was for me. And even if I had, I wouldn't be able to go anyway, because I actually already have plans with *my* gang that day, and we're actually doing even more secret fun stuff than you, but unlike you, we're actually keeping it secret!"

And then I turn on my heel and storm out of the form room. I hear Amelia saying, "Yeah, right. Liar," after me, and Natalie murmuring something that sounds like it might be, "Leave it." But I don't look back.

I run straight to a toilet, lock myself in a cubicle and cry for about five minutes. I don't think anybody knows. I can't believe I thought Natalie wanted me in their gang. I can't believe how disappointed I feel that she doesn't. I thought I was tough now. I thought I had become cool and independent. *What's wrong with me?*

I come out of the cubicle and wash my face in the sink with cold water. I feel slightly better. *I want to*

be cool and independent. I dry my face and look at myself in the mirror. You can tell I've been crying. *I want to be cool and independent.* I stare at my face until it starts to look more normal again. I am *going* to be cool and independent.

The bell goes for registration. OK. I am going to be cool and independent. Right after I organise a spontaneous secret gang outing for the weekend.

Honestly, it is much harder to organise a spontaneous secret gang outing at the weekend than you might imagine.

I try Shantair and Cherry at chess club after school that day, but they're both busy already. Cherry has a clarinet exam on Saturday, and Shantair has a drama rehearsal. They don't change their minds even when I say we could do anything they want, cinema, bouncy castle, anything. They just tell me I don't listen and that I've "missed the point".

I have no luck with Tanya the next day when I'm finally able to give her the hell cartoon I made for her at break time, after our maths lesson.

"Oh, Toons, that is *epic*, epic!" She thumps me on the back, and I try not to sway.

"So what about Saturday?" I ask her, as people file past us.

"Can't. I'm grounded, innit. Thanks to that stupid, *set up* detention."

"Oh, no," I say. I'm about to say, "Can't you sneak out? Or offer to do the hoovering or something?" when Tanya surprises me by saying, "Right, I'm off to the library."

"You're off to the … library?" I say carefully, trying not to sound offensively surprised.

"Yeah, 'course," replies Tanya. "Got to photocopy this, haven't I?" She waves my school-hell cartoon at me.

"You're … *photocopying* it?"

"Yeah. For deffo. Think I'll start with a hundred. What do you reckon? I'm going to put this all round school. That'll show them. No one gives Tanya 'the beef' Harris detention and gets away with it." And then she struts off down the corridor.

Oh *my*! Thank goodness I didn't put my name on it … Wow. I really hope that doesn't get me into trouble … I mean, no one knows I did it apart from Tanya … *hmmm*.

In art, I ask Emily, Megan and Fatimah. They are my last chance, and unbelievably none of them want to go on a spontaneous secret gang outing. Or are busy. *Whatever*.

"It's my weekend with my dad," explains Emily, looking pained (and to be fair, like she actually would have loved to come). "Otherwise I won't see him for another two weeks."

I suddenly feel bad. "Oh, no, that's cool. Don't worry about it at all," I say. "We'll do another one, when you're free."

I mean, actually that's what this should really be about, isn't it? Planning stuff and hanging out with the people you like. (When they *are* free.) Not about getting revenge. What have I become? Amelia has really brought out my evil side.

"Oh, yes! Let's do another one!" squeals Megan, who is also visiting her dad.

"I'd love that!" chimes in Fatimah, who has to go to see her cousins in Manchester.

"It's a deal," I say, and we do our special handshake.

Terry and Joshua watch us suspiciously, but don't say anything.

CHAPTER 10

Saturday comes around all too quickly, and I have no plans and no one to hang out with. Ryan has been in trouble twice this morning already, once for making too much noise, and once for getting his toys everywhere again.

I join my mum in the kitchen where she is soaking some dried lentils and some dried chickpeas in different bowls. (Yes, we've reached the legumes stage of the economy drive.) I'm sure my mum will have to go shopping soon. There can't be that much food *left* in the cupboards.

I survey my mum and the lentils for a moment. "So, um, is the economy drive nearly over?" I ask her.

"Oh, not you *as well*, Jessica," snaps Mum. "This is hard enough without your constant complaints."

"I wasn't complaining, I was just—"

"I'M A SPACEMAN! I'M A SPACEMAN! I'M A SPACEMAN! I'M A SPACEMAN!" Ryan comes running into the kitchen, hitting the cupboards with a bat, and effectively interrupting me.

"Ryan! Shut up!" I shriek, annoyed. Ryan runs back out again.

"Don't shout, please, Jessica," says my mum wearily. Then, "Your brother is driving me *mad*."

"Tell me about it," I mutter.

"Why don't you take him when you go out today?"

"I'm not going out today."

"I thought you were going to the cinema with your friends?"

"Oh, I was, but none of them were free in the end."

"Not even Natalie?" My mum looks away from what she is doing long enough to give me a piercing stare. "How is she, by the way? We haven't seen her here for *ages* now."

"Yes, I suppose it has been a while." I stare back.

"Any particular reason for that?" asks my mum, still staring.

I contemplate telling her about the whole thing, but really that's a no go. She is liable to do one of two interfering things. She will either: (a) Take Natalie's side and make me apologise; or (b) Take my side, ring Lisa and then make Natalie apologise. I can't let either of those things happen.

"No, no particular reason," I reply evenly.

My mum looks like she doesn't believe me, but decides not to press it. She turns her attention back to the soaking pulses. "Do give her my love, won't you?" she says pointedly.

"Yeah, yeah," I reply tiredly. *Natalie doesn't want your love*, I think. *She's too busy being mean.*

"Well then, why *don't* you take Ryan out and do something with him instead?" suggests my mum.

Ha. Yes, I see, very clever. Get me to do your parenting job for you? No chance. "I don't think so," I say.

"I'M A SPACEMAN! I'M A SPACEMAN! I'M A SPACEMAN! I'M A SPACEMAN!" Ryan comes running back in, hitting the cupboards again.

"RYAN! OUT!" screams my mum.

I jump. Ryan runs away. "Let me put it this way," says my mum, turning back to me. "You are going out, and you are taking Ryan. And you had better not come back for at least three hours. I need him out from under my feet."

This is just so *typical*. I can't believe I have to take Ryan out on *my* Saturday. And as if that's not bad enough, I didn't even get to choose where we went, Ryan did. How unfair is that?

I suggested the park, as I figured Ryan could run off some of his excess energy, but Ryan insisted on seeing a new film at the cinema, and my mum even gave us money to shut him up. *Money!* During an economy drive! (And to think *I* wasn't even allowed a badgemaker!)

I suppose I should just be grateful that we managed to talk him out of taking all the things he wanted to bring along. Initially, he wanted his space helmet, his bat *and* his Winnie the Pooh bear. (The combination of which, frankly, made him look insane.) We convinced him to leave the bat. But he insisted Winnie the Pooh wanted to see the film as well. Finally my mum got the helmet off him and told him he'd have to tell Winnie the Pooh all about the film later. Nightmare.

Now we're at the mall, and I'm just terrified we're going to bump into CAC and they're going to see for sure that I lied about having a brilliant secret gang activity, and that I am instead hanging out with my six-year-old brother as if he is my only friend.

"Hey, Jessica." I whirl round and see Joshua standing next to the ice cream.

"Oh, er, hi," I say, relieved he isn't anyone else. It's weird seeing him out of his school uniform. For some reason he looks older in jeans and a T-shirt.

"Who are you?" demands Ryan.

"I'm Joshua," says Joshua. "I like your badge," he adds, clocking the ACE astronaut cartoon badge I made for Ryan. (Ryan insisted on wearing that out. It seemed small fry compared to the rest.)

"I'm a *spaceman*," says Ryan proudly. "My sister made it."

"She's very talented," says Joshua, smiling at me.

"Only at drawing," says Ryan, which at least does make Joshua and me laugh.

I'm waiting for an opportunity to say, "OK then, see you later," but somehow we end up chatting. Not only that, but Ryan starts quizzing Joshua about space stuff, and they sort of, well, *hit it off*. I'm secretly starting to wonder if I can leave them to it and have a quick look round the shops.

But before I know it, Ryan is leading us over to the board with the film listings on it, we have discovered we have nearly an hour to wait until the next film and Ryan has invited Joshua to watch it with us.

"Ryan, Joshua doesn't want to watch a stupid kids' film with us," I say.

"I don't mind, actually," says Joshua. "I'm not meeting my friends till later. Just wanted to get out of the house. Only if you don't mind, though?" He seems to be asking me.

"Of course she doesn't mind," says Ryan.

"No, cool," I say, "as long as you don't think you'll be bored."

We get the tickets and then ponder what to do next. Ryan spots a couple snogging a few metres away, and says, "Urgh,

109

they're *kissing*. Germs." Joshua and I giggle. Spurred on by us laughing, Ryan suddenly shouts, "Oi! *Get a room!*"

The couple jump and look round in surprise. "Ryan!" I say, pulling him away. "Where did you even *hear* that?"

"Probably that bloody television," says Ryan mildly, actually doing quite an accurate impression of my mum.

I try desperately not to laugh. "Ryan, stop showing off," I say firmly. I mean, it *is* funny, but six is probably a bit young to behave like such a hooligan.

"Nah, I don't think I'll be *bored*," says Joshua.

I feel like I'd better get Ryan out of here though, in case the couple realise it was him, or he shouts at someone else. I think Joshua reads my mind.

"Hey, I know this place that does slush puppies downstairs, since we have some time to kill," he says.

"Perfect," I say, and we start moving.

I briefly wonder how much time Joshua spends at the mall, as he seems to know where everything is. (He even gets mildly irked when we see a sign for a coffee shop that he swears doesn't exist.) But mainly he is quite laid-back.

As we head downstairs, chatting and joking, I become aware that I'm actually, sort of, having *fun*. I relax a little bit. Joshua is quite funny. He has this cheeky, rude streak, which in turn brings out my cheeky, rude streak. More than usual.

"There's another one," says Joshua, pointing at a sign that says Tall, Dark and Coffee. "I wonder where that café is?"

"Your bum," I joke, making Ryan giggle.

"I'd be surprised if it was," says Joshua innocently, playing along. Ryan giggles some more.

Joshua insists on trying to find Tall, Dark and Coffee. We follow all the signs for it and go round in a circle twice. Ryan starts to get irritable. "I thought we were getting slushies?" he whines.

Joshua wisely starts to bail. "OK, I give up," he says. "We'll go get slushies."

"Well, we'll just have to assume it *was* your bum, then," I say, nodding sagely. They both laugh.

The Slush Pile is quite busy, but we manage to get a table and spend some enjoyable time hanging out. Joshua and I keep jokily being rude to each other. I'm kind of winning, so to get me back Joshua burps loudly and then goes, "Jessica!" as if it had been *me*. The nerve. But it was funny. Ryan nearly fell off his chair he was laughing so much.

Even the film that we watch isn't that bad for a kids' film. I don't know if I should admit this, but it actually made me laugh out loud twice. (Although I totally saw the ending coming a mile off.)

As we troop back out, with Ryan repeating the word "awesome" indiscriminately to describe every bit of the film, I realise I've actually had a really good day.

Joshua spies his friends on our way out of the cinema, and waves at a group of about ten lads. I recognise them from school. I think half of them are in the basketball team (ooh, including Joe and Daniel) but they're dressed just like Joshua, in jeans. They wave back and shout, "Oi oi!" at him.

My good mood nearly vanishes, and I instantly feel nervous. I'm not entirely sure why. I mean, it's not like I'm *scared* of boys. It's not even that I *dislike* them or anything. I just don't hang around them that much. And it has tended to be boys more than girls that have shouted stuff at me in the past (like "Oooh

112

chess club"). And it's usually massive groups of boys that shout rather than just one or two. Oh *God*, I hope they don't shout at me in front of Joshua and Ryan. That would be sooo embarrassing.

Joshua greets them with what look to me like even better secret handshakes than the one that ACE invented. They even pat each other on the back and kind of half hug. I'm just thinking that maybe I can copy this and slightly revamp ACE's handshake, when one of them says, "And who's this then?" I immediately tense up.

"Oh, this is Jessica," says Joshua. "You know, from school."

"And I'm Ryan, Jessica's brother," pipes up Ryan, not to be sidelined.

The group of boys look us up and down. "What's that on your badge?" one of them asks Ryan.

"It's a spaceman," says Ryan, glancing at the badge proudly. "My sister made it for me," he adds.

The lads glance between us some more. I can't work out if they are about to be really mean or not. Then one of them suddenly says, "Hang on, are you *Toons*?"

They all stare at me. I'm not sure what to reply.

Before I can, one of them says, "She is. I've seen her with Tanya Harris. You're Toons, aren't you?"

"Um," I manage. (Why do they all know my nickname?)

"Did you draw *this*?" One of them, called Michael, whips a piece of paper from his pocket. It's a photocopy of the cartoon I did of our school.

Ohhhh. Realisation dawns. Tanya has circulated it around school already. And she's told everyone "Toons" did it! Blimey!

"Er, yes, I did that," I say.

"*Nice one!*" exclaims Michael.

Then, two things happen at once. Firstly, the boys get really excited, keep grinning at each other and start high-fiving me. (I don't mean to boast, but it's honestly as if they've discovered I'm *Banksy* or something.) And secondly CAC all troop out of the cinema, having watched their film.

114

Which means that, as CAC *Best Day Ever* enter the cinema foyer, they see me being high-fived, patted on the back, and generally congratulated by half of our year's basketball team.

I know that if I want to be strong and independent and stuff, this is exactly the sort of thing that I shouldn't care about. But I can't help it. This event elevates today to *best day ever*.

CHAPTER 11

Ah, life is good. As Ryan and I enter our house later that day, there is a delicious smell of curry wafting all around.

"What time do you call this?" says my mum, instead of "Hello" or even "Thank you for taking my nightmare child out for the day." "I was just about to ring you. Dinner is on the table now."

Honestly. First she wants us out, and then she's annoyed about it. There's no pleasing some people. Luckily I am way too Zen to rise to the bait.

"Blimey, Mum, there's no pleasing you, is there?" I reply. (Well, all right, *nearly* too Zen.)

"Sorry, love," she says. "I was just worried about you. Thanks for taking Ryan out. You're a good girl really." She kisses me on the head, and we all sit down to dinner.

"And I'm good, too," Ryan adds, apparently feeling left out.

"From the sounds of things, you were a blimmin' nuisance this morning," says my dad, dishing out rice to everyone.

"Well, boys will be boys," says my mum. "Have you calmed down now, sweet pea?" My mum looks at Ryan fondly, seemingly suffering from acute memory loss. It's as if she has no actual recollection of the spaceman row earlier.

To my delight, this meal is delicious. My mum's made two different curries. One is apparently called Tarka Dahl, and has loads of lentils in it. The chickpea one is called Chana Masala. It tastes amazing.

"Mum, this tastes amazing," I say with my mouth full. I swallow. "This is my favourite meal of the economy drive, bar none."

"Well, good," says my mum, looking pleased. "It certainly took the longest."

We all start chatting about the film, which means that Ryan goes into an excited monologue while my parents nod and say, "Oh yes?" and exchange little smiles with each other because of how cute he looks when he's animated. We all seem really happy for once.

This is certainly the happiest I've felt for *ages*. I'm still reliving how awesome it was when half the basketball team congratulated me! It was such an amazing feeling. And *Amelia's face*! Priceless. I sigh contentedly.

I *knew* I was brilliant. But to be honest, I didn't actually expect anyone else to cotton on to it until I was a famous and eccentric cartoonist in my fifties. I kind of weirdly had this vague fantasy of being "interesting" and elusive, and growing whatever the female equivalent of a beard is … still a beard, I suppose … but anyway. I have peaked forty years ahead of schedule. Which is weird.

Anyway, it doesn't matter. I'm *famous* (in a roundabout way to upwards of fifty people). This is the coolest thing that's ever happened. I feel like I can do anything now. I can take on the world. Nothing matters.

I sort of don't ever want this day to end. I want it to

stay being the day where the brilliant thing happened *forever*.

 My leg starts to vibrate gently and I realise I still have my phone in my pocket. I pull it out discreetly, and try to look at it under the table (my parents are very anti-mobile phones at the dinner table). But luckily they are still entranced by Ryan's enthusiastic film review.

I click on it. I have a message from Natalie!

How U been? Wot U up 2 l8r? X

What? I read it again. Then I read it again, just to make sure. It's hard to do this and still be discreet.

"Jessica? What are you doing?" asks my dad.

"Nothing," I murmur, shoving the phone back in my pocket and returning my attention to the dinner table. Well, some of my attention. My mind is racing.

What the what? My first thought is that maybe she got the wrong number and that message was meant for someone else. I mean, that type of thing has happened before. Mainly in note form, but still. Accidentally or deliberately, it seems a bit odd that she would suddenly message me out of the blue. I'm just going to ignore it. I'm not going to fall for that again.

On my way up to my room after dinner, my phone buzzes again. I sit down in my room and read another text message from Natalie.

Hey Jess. RU free 2nite sweets? Wondered if U wanted 2 hang out. X

OK, that one had my name. It is overtly definitely meant for me. I still can't rule out the possibility of a trick … Actually, you know what? I really can't be bothered with this. It's ridiculous. I had a great day today. I am going to continue to feel good, and be myself, and not get bogged down in trying to second-guess what Natalie is thinking. Ha.

I put my phone down and start sorting through some of the clean washing that my mum has left on my bed. My phone starts ringing. I check the screen, bewildered. Natalie is *ringing* me. She hasn't rung me in … well, *ages*.

Curious, I answer. "Hello?"

"Jessica!" comes Natalie's voice. "Babes, I'm so

glad you answered. When you didn't reply to my texts I was worried you might have changed your number or something. How are you?"

"Um, fine … um … why are you ringing me?"

"What kind of question is that? Uh, like, 'cause I'm your best friend? Look, everything's got stupid, Jess. We need to sort all this out, you and me."

I can't believe it. Those are the words I've being dying to hear since we fell out (although, to be honest, in my fantasy version she's way more apologetic than that) and yet, now it's finally happened, I don't care. I really don't care.

"Natalie, why are you so bothered about being my friend now?" I say. "You've been totally excluding me at school."

"Look, I know, things have got really weird. I haven't exactly enjoyed the last couple of weeks, either."

"Ha!" I blurt. "Yeah, right!" (Maybe I slightly care. But only about the truth and justice of it all.) "You looked like you were having a great time. And you and Amelia started all this anyway."

"Look, I know, I know. I haven't entirely been completely nice to you. And I'm really sorry about that." (Wow – she actually did apologise.) "I just find it hard to fit everybody in at the moment."

"What does that mean?" I ask.

"I don't know, I just – I really like you. You're my best friend and you always will be. But I really like Amelia as well, and you guys don't get on, and I get caught in the middle, and it's hard."

"I have always been perfectly nice to Amelia," I say crossly. "She hates me, Nat. She's always picking on me, and making little comments, and putting me down. She's the one causing any tension, not me."

"I know, I know." Natalie sighs. "I know that's how it looks, but she's new, it's hard for her. She's just like that because she's jealous of you."

"*WHAT?*" (OK, I didn't mean to shout that.) But I feel kind of incredulous. "What's she jealous of, Nat? My rubbish, dog-sick jacket? Maybe my terrible immaturity? Is that it?"

"She's jealous of you and me. Every time she wants to do something together, you have a story about some time you and me already did it, and had loads of fun, and … you can be a bit tactless, and I told her that's just how you are, but for some reason she started doing it back to you."

Oh. My. God. Information overload. So much I want to reply to. I am *not* tactless. I can't believe Amelia thinks I've been doing to her what she's been doing to me. (I mean since before I started deliberately trying to do it to her.) I gasp. I'm momentarily speechless as I process all this.

"Well," I say finally. "The bottom line is, you chose her, didn't you? You chose her over me. She got what she wanted. So that's that, really." I feel surprisingly close to tears.

"No, that isn't that!" squeals Natalie. "Stop being such a blimmin' drama queen! I'm allowed to have more than one friend. Look, I didn't *choose* her at all, Jess. It just happened that way at the time, and then it was really hard to come back from without losing face."

"Losing face? Nat, you could never lose face with me. I'm the least street person ever."

"I know!" Natalie laughs and sniffs, and I wonder if she's slightly crying. "Look, I know I should have been honest with you ages ago, but I've been a bit jealous of you and the chess club, and when Amelia suggested this gang, it seemed like the perfect way to give you a taste of your own medicine and—"

"Whoa, whoa, whoa," I interrupt. "Back up there, *you've* been *jealous* of the *chess club*? You hate the chess club!"

"Only because you love it so much!"

"I don't love it; it's OK and I like chess. Like I said, I'm not a very street person."

Natalie splutters with laughter. "I've missed you so much. Do you want to come round to my house tonight? We could talk about this, and hang out. Maybe have a sleepover?"

Natalie, my beloved best friend, sounds really upset and genuine. But I still feel so hurt by everything, that I say, "Won't Amelia be there?" slightly sneeringly.

"No. Look, Amelia's great, but we don't hang out all the time. I miss you, Jess. You're so funny, and Amelia's mostly quite serious. I miss our silly jokes together. Those cartoons you drew of your gang were amazing. I was well impressed." I feel myself relenting. Natalie pauses. I hear another sniff. "Have you missed *me*?" she adds quietly.

"Maybe," I hear myself say.

"Oh my God, come round right now!" she exclaims.

"Ask your mum to drive you over. We have to make up properly. I want to hug you. I can't do that over the phone."

"Um …" I hesitate.

"I never watched that dinosaur programme," continues Natalie. "We could watch it together if you come round. And bake the dinosaur biscuits! I'll check my mum has flour … Oh my God, I found that poem you wrote the other day, about MBlaze." (Oh yeah, I forgot about that – Natalie and I used to write poems to MBlaze, but instead of being about us loving them, they were offering MBlaze tips on how to become more normal.) "It was so funny! Oh, *please* come round!"

"Um …" I need to think about this properly. Should I go round there? Do I want to be Natalie's friend again? Twenty-four hours ago this was my dream. And now it's really happened. Natalie wants me back. And I love Natalie … I do. I *do* want to go round there! Excitement surges through me as I realise this. Everything's going to be OK. Everything's—

"And I tell you what," Natalie starts gabbling excitedly, "the first thing we can talk about is how you met the basketball team and why they were all

I'm BRILLIANT!

high-fiving you. How much gossip have I missed here?"

Oh. *Ohhhhh*. Of course. I feel like I've just come crashing back down to earth. Natalie doesn't want me back. She just wants to hear about the basketball team. I am just a means to an end. I suppose I looked "cool" enough to be her friend again, did I? Now she cares so much about "losing face" and boys stuff. *Ohhh*.

Well, I'm not cool. (I'm *brilliant*, but I'm not cool.) I refuse to be used and then cast aside again.

"Yeah, well," I say. "It's great that you want to hang out and everything, Nat, but we're in rival gangs now. Maybe you should have thought a bit more about that before excluding me." Then I hang up.

CHAPTER 12

There's nothing like some lovely, clement weather to cheer the days along. And this is *nothing* like some lovely, clement weather to cheer the days along. Ha ha, I am still funny. (I am a humorous cartoonist.)

It's been raining for pretty much three whole days now. *Honestly*. What is the point of springtime if it's just going to rain? Come on, universe, don't you think it's about time you stopped making it rain? (I don't ask for me, but you should see Ryan when he hasn't been able to run off his excess energy. Maybe we ought to get him a hamster wheel.)

I'm feeling weirdly upbeat despite the dreary weather and occasional domestic flare-ups, though. I sort of don't care about anything. The future seems like it might contain good things, even if bad things are still happening sometimes as well. I think I've sort of relaxed slightly in general.

It's like, now that one good thing has happened to me (i.e. I have drawn a cartoon that is officially popular) I know that it is possible that other good things could happen. I don't need to worry so much about the little things. Like who is calling who back and that sort of thing.

Natalie hasn't called me since I hung up on her. Not that I care. I'm not really thinking about Natalie much any more. Officially. I mean, I'm thinking about her a tiny bit, but that's not my fault. I mean, it's impossible to erase memories or think of nothing, isn't it?

Ohh. All right, I have sort of been thinking about her a lot. (Maybe even, what you could describe as "non-stop", if you wanted.) Because part of me thinks I might have overreacted, but part of me thinks I sort of had to do what I did for the principle. I mean, otherwise it's like Natalie can just pick me up and put me down whenever she feels like it. And that isn't right.

So apart from not quite being able to work out

if I am overreacting or if my stance is justified, everything is fine. Well, Natalie and Amelia have gone back to frostily ignoring me in the form room again. But apart from *that*, everything is fine.

Well, also, there was a notice in assembly on Monday about not wasting paper, or the "privilege" of the photocopier might be taken away (which I think might indirectly be because of my hell-school cartoon). *How unbelievable is that?* I am equally thrilled and scared of the repercussions of my kind-of-but-not-really notoriety. Anyway, the point is, apart from *all of that*, everything is fine.

And anyway. Things aren't all doom and gloom. I have actually sort of made a new friend. Joshua has gone from boy-who-I-sat-next-to-in-art-that-I-thought-was-funny-but-who-probably-thought-I-was-weird, to boy-who-I-sit-next-to-in-art-that-is-my-friend-and-may-or-may-not-think-I-am-weird-but-it-doesn't-matter-anyway.

Which is pretty good progress. I mean, I don't *want* to lose my old friends. But if I *am* going to, it is at least nice to know that I am in fact capable of making new ones.

We exchanged numbers on Saturday. And on Monday night he texted me, joking about the assembly warning about my cartoon, and how I was an outlaw, and he was going to "shop me to the feds". He really makes me laugh.

And now it's Tuesday and it's art again! I *love* art. I have always looked forward to it the most out of all my subjects. But now I'm better friends with everyone I sit with, it's even more fun. I'm almost *excited* about the prospect of Tuesday's lesson. (And I mean, it is still *school*. Weird.)

We have to draw a big vase that has been put on our table. Other tables have jugs and stuff. (We are supposed to concentrate on making it look round and three-dimensional.) Then Mrs Cooper goes into the little side staffroom to "make a cup of tea". So we are left to it!

It's brilliant, we get to joke around while we draw! Terry and Fatimah tell funny stories about their weekends, and Joshua and

Emily chip in with funny interruptions. It's a laugh. Then they start talking about being able to get into fifteen-certificate films and Terry asserts he would definitely be able to do it.

"Urgh, you said 'do it'," I joke, and they all laugh (apart from Terry).

"What? I would," Terry maintains.

"What, you would *do it*?" I ask.

"Yeah, I would definitely *do it*," says Terry. More laughter.

"*Urgh*, Terry wants to *do it*," I tease. Emily, Megan and Fatimah giggle.

"Oh, grow up," says Joshua, pretending to tell me off, but still looking amused.

"What? Oh, I get it!" says Terry. "Do it. Yeah." Then he turns behind him and shouts, "Oi, Dan! Do you know how to *do it*?"

Dan replies, "Yes thanks."

And Terry goes, "Urgh, Dan knows how to *do it*!" I think the subtlety of the joke is getting lost somewhat, but it does make quite a few people laugh. So much so that Mrs Cooper comes back into the room to demand what all the noise is about.

As she walks in, Terry is doing a weird victory

dance in his seat which Mrs Cooper immediately clocks.

"Terry! Stand up this instant! What on earth is going on in here?"

The room falls silent, and Terry stands up, contrite and apologetic. I can't help myself. I move his stool back a foot. I think he'll notice, but he doesn't. When Mrs Cooper tells him to sit back down, he does an amazing comedy pratfall straight on to the floor. The class erupts.

Eventually Mrs Cooper restores order and then really tells me off for moving the stool. I feel a bit bad, actually, but I still think it was worth it. It was *really* funny. And he *is* a joke thief.

Oh, I love art. I wish I could stay there forever. But I can't. I have to go to other lessons and be given evils by CAC if I happen to make eye contact with any of them. It would be much better for everyone if my whole timetable was art. I mean, imagine how many cartoons about the school being like hell I would be able to get done then?

"We make a good team, you and me, don't we,

Toons?" says Tanya, catching me at lunch. "Oh my life! What about that assembly? Bare jokes. We should do more. You any good with spray paint?"

"Um …" I falter, faintly worried. "I've never really tried." Which is true.

"We should try it out sometime. You'll be needing a tag for your gang anyway, won't you?"

Ha! Yeah, *as if* my gang that does battles with badgemakers needs a proper graffiti-on-a-public-wall signature that tells the police we've been by. Oh my goodness! I absolutely cannot get involved in proper tagging and spray paint graffiti. For one thing, my mum would kill me. And for another thing, my mum would kill me.

"I don't know, Tanya," I say, pretending to consider this. "I feel like I work better on paper at the moment; that's what I really want to concentrate on."

"Suit yourself," she replies quite amicably.

Ah, well. I have at least enjoyed my few heady days of feeling like a rebel because of a cartoon someone else told me to draw. But now I have been reminded that, in reality, I am actually quite scared of authority.

When I get back to 6C at the end of lunch, there is another piece of posh white card on my desk. This time it's an envelope with "To Jessica" written on it in swirly writing with one of those cool silver pens they sell in Smiths that I really want to get.

I glance up at Natalie and Amelia. They are sitting with the rest of CAC a couple of metres away. They see me pick up the envelope but they're pretending to be nonchalant and ignore me. I wonder what it says. *Ohh*. I hope not something really horrible.

I open it, and to my surprise, inside is an *invitation*. An invitation to a CAC outing: bowling on Sunday! I'm invited? *I'm invited!* I scroll down, the letter talks about Natalie hoping we can all be friends! I'm *included*! (So she doesn't mind that I hung up on her.) Oh my God, this is amazing!

"Hey, guys, I think I can make this," I call out

excitedly, waving the letter at them. I can't help but grin. We can all finally be friends.

They take one look at me and then burst out laughing. I freeze. That's not good. "Are you *sure,* Jessica?" asks Natalie coldly. "Have you read it properly?"

"Um," I say, trying to reread the letter but feeling too nervous to be able to take in any of the words. I feel really hot.

"Are you definitely free *that* day?" adds Amelia.

I look at the date. It's *last* Sunday. They have given me an invitation to a past event. I was never invited. Embarrassment and mortification wash over me.

Well, I have to hand it to them: they have raised my expectations and then dashed them spectacularly.

CHAPTER 13

I'm not going to lie to you. I'm angry. I am very angry. I am *livid*, in fact. I feel hot under the collar every time I think about it. I *can't believe* they did that.

The injustice of it! I sit there seething through my afternoon science and history lessons. How *dare* they do that! I am *not* some idiot that's desperate to hang out with them. How *dare* they make it look like I am. If anything, I was doing *brilliantly* without them.

OK, I *know* I hung up on Natalie, and that's mean. But that is no reason to pull something like *this* on me.

Ohh. I can't believe they did this. I can't believe they made me look so stupid. Maybe I should just rise above it and not even react. I mean, that might annoy them more than trying to retaliate. They probably *want* me to be upset.

Yeah, that's it. I'm going to rise above it. Leave them to their silly games. I know I'm not a bad person. *I* know I don't want to go on their stupid outings. I mean, obviously, there was a time when I *did*, but I don't any more. And I didn't when they tricked me with that stupid letter.

I don't have to care about their nonsense. I'm just going to rise above it and ignore it. I finish my last lesson feeling slightly better. I'm above this. I don't need to care.

I have to walk past CAC on my way out of the form room. "Hey, you should really open your post on time," comments Cassy as I pass. Amelia giggles.

"Yeah, we would have loved you to come otherwise," says Amelia.

I feel my temperature rising, but I am determined to keep my cool. "I think you are all really out of order," I say calmly.

They think I'm immature, do they? Well, listen to this – I'm going to sound like a *grown-up*. "I'm not even angry, I'm just disappointed," I add.

I glance at Natalie, who won't catch my eye. "Natalie, how could you let them do this?"

"*Natalie, how could you let them do this?*" Amelia imitates me, but making me sound like a whiny baby.

I feel my temperature rising, but I ignore Amelia and continue to address Natalie. "I thought you said you wanted to be my friend."

"*Aw, be my fwend …*" Amelia and Cassy continue to impersonate me. Natalie still won't look at me.

"Nat—"

"*Whatever*, Jessica. It's like you said, isn't it? We're in rival gangs, after all." Natalie interrupts me and gives me a filthy look. (I'm going to go out on a limb here and say that I think she's still quite annoyed I hung up on her.)

It's more than that, though. The thing is, the more I think about it, the more I'm worried I might have overreacted that day, now I look back on it. The rest of the phone conversation did seem genuine, and now I wonder if Natalie really was reaching out to me and is now understandably annoyed that I rejected her. But I can't exactly explain that now, or take it back, can I? And it still doesn't justify *this*.

"All right, fine," I say, feeling my temperature

138

rising further. I really hope I'm not bright red. Calm thoughts. I am calm. "If that's how you want it to be. Enjoy the rest of your life." I turn and walk away from them.

Hmm. OK. Well, I think I very nearly *did* rise above it. Kind of slightly fell at the last rising-above-it hurdle. We can probably all agree that the rising above it plan hasn't one hundred per cent worked. I *think* I may need to address this now. But what can I do?

So. What has two thumbs and no plan of attack or revenge of any kind? *This guy.* You can't see me, but I am pointing at myself with my thumbs – but subtly: I'm on the bus home. I don't want to make a fool of myself. I have a whole gang of people specially to do that for me. Ha. Aaagghh.

God, I feel miserable as I enter my house. But something is different. There is no smell of dinner being nearly ready. I clock a rucksack sitting at the bottom of the stairs. My sister's rucksack. My sister – my sister is home! I love my sister!

"Tammy? Tammy?" I call out.

"In here," comes Mum's voice.

I enter the kitchen excitedly, but find my mum, dad and sister all looking angry, and apparently mid-discussion. No one seems pleased to see me.

"Well, let's not— Look, we can talk about this later," says my mum to Tammy. "Your father and I need to crack on with dinner."

"Oh how *convenient*," says Tammy, her voice heavy with sarcasm. (Why is Tammy ignoring me? Say hello!)

"Tammy!" I say. "Well, don't look too pleased to see me, then."

"It's not *you* I'm not pleased to see," says Tammy. I go over and hug her. Tammy adds to my mum over my shoulder, "Whatever you do, don't let helping the world get in the way of domesticity, will you?"

My mum turns away and starts muttering angrily to my dad. I catch the words "living end" but not much else.

"Say it to my face," says Tammy. "Or why don't we put it to a family vote?"

"Don't you *dare*," hisses my mum. (I have no idea what is going on, but Tammy appears to have really angered my parents.)

"Now, look here, Tammy," begins my dad.

"Jessica—" says Tammy.

"No," interrupts my dad.

"Jessica, how would you like to have a lovely pet dog?" asks Tammy.

"Really? I would love that!" I say.

"No," says my dad.

"I'm involved with a rescue shelter and we really need to find homes for the dogs. But Mum and Dad here don't seem to want to take one. They said it would be too big an adjustment for the family. But you'd like it, wouldn't you? I think everyone should vote. Where's Ryan?"

"*No*," says my dad again.

"Oh, can we? Can we please have a dog?" I ask excitedly. "They need rescuing. *Please?*"

Tammy folds her arms across her chest and looks at my mum with a very smug expression on her face. My mum looks like she wants to murder Tammy. "This really is the *living end*," she says.

My dad catches my mum's look and changes tack. "How about a nice cup of tea?" he says.

Well, eventually the shouting dies down and my parents make us pasta. We're still on the economy drive. ("*Which is just one of the many reasons it would*  *be ludicrous to get a dog.*" They sent me to my room after dinner, but I could still pretty much hear everything.)

Having a dog would be great. I could train it to attack Amelia. I fantasise about that for a moment, then there's a knock at my bedroom door and Tammy comes in.

"Hey, Jess, sorry about all the commotion," she says, and flops on to my bed. (Though, to be honest, while it was happening, Tammy looked like she very much enjoyed being at the centre of a shouting match.) "It's a shame our parents are so short-sighted," she adds, sighing.

"Yeah," I say uncertainly. "Um, are they?"

"God, yeah." Tammy exhales again. "They're just myopic."

"What does myopic mean?"

"It means short-sighted."

"Right, yeah." I nod, trying to look thoughtful.

"How are you, anyway? Still cartooning? Ryan loves his badge just a bit, eh?"

Oh, I *love* my sister. I love it when she comes home. (Apart from the shouting, obviously.) Suddenly I'm just talking away to her, going on about cartoons, and she seems really interested. I show her a photocopy of the hell-school one and she *loves* it.

"I am so impressed with you, Jessica," she says. "Sticking it to The Man. Good for you."

Hmm. I'm not sure I can say that that was *exactly* what I was doing with that cartoon. "Well, it was Tanya Harris's idea," I tell her.

"Tanya Harris sounds great. Stick with her," says Tammy.

"Yeah," I say uncertainly. Though part of me wants to laugh at that statement.

"Anyway, what happened to Natalie? I thought she was your best friend?"

"Oh, well. That's a long story."

"I'm all ears," says Tammy.

So I tell Tammy the whole sorry mess, about the falling-out, and the gangs, and Joshua and the basketball team. I even tell her about the mean trick with the letter. I wasn't sure I was going to mention that. I'm still kind of embarrassed about it. Tammy listens to the whole thing patiently, occasionally saying, "Oh yes," or "Good for you," until I am finished.

"And the thing is, Tammy, I just don't know what I can do about it."

"Well now," says Tammy, pausing for effect. "You have the key to what you can do about it right here."

"What do you mean?" I ask.

"You've got to play to your strengths. You are a cartoonist. Don't underestimate the power of a satirical cartoon. That's one of the great ways the masses can undermine The Man. The workers can bring down the system. You have power at your fingertips."

OK, I keep hearing people say stuff like this, especially with all the protests and financial stuff going on. I don't fully understand it, but apparently 1% of the population control or own all the wealth of the other 99%. We (the masses) are the 99% and we should totally get our way with stuff because there are more of us. But, the 1% ("The Man") are in charge, so they make everything suit them.

Tammy seems convinced the masses can

undermine The Man with a satirical cartoon, but no one ever fully explains *how*. And as far as I can tell a satirical cartoon is just a cartoon making fun of the bad things that corrupt, important people do. But the corrupt, important people are normally so rich they probably don't care anyway.

"Do you really reckon?" I say, unconvinced.

"Totally. Amelia is like a dictator. If you mock her, and laugh at her, her followers will lose faith in her and she will lose her power."

"That *sounds* brilliant," I say cautiously.

"Because it *is* brilliant," Tammy assures me. "I'll leave you to it. Get cracking." And she leaves my bedroom.

I hear her walk along the corridor to Ryan's room. "Razza! My main man! How would you like a dog?"

145

CHAPTER 14

Hmm. OK. A satirical cartoon. A satirical cartoon about Amelia. Could that work? Is it even a good idea? I love my sister, but she does seem to enjoy and gravitate towards conflict and drama a bit.

I mean, if I made a cartoon about Amelia, surely that's nearly as bad as her encouraging everyone to bully me in the first place? I mean, doesn't that count as *stirring*? What if it makes everything worse? Plus, I really have no idea how to go about doing it.

I remember seeing a political cartoon in history once. It was about how in the lead-up to the Second World War, the Allies let Hitler do loads of stuff he wasn't supposed to that broke treaties or contracts or something. The cartoon I saw showed a broken wall being fixed with a giant piece of paper that said "*I will be good, signed Adolf Hitler*," and the caption at the bottom read: "*Our new defence*".

I really liked that cartoon. Apparently, it was because Prime Minister Chamberlain (who was a bit of a softie) thought if he got Hitler to sign a treaty promising peace, war could be avoided. But Hitler didn't care about the treaties, 'cause he didn't mean it, and he kept doing stuff anyway. (A bit like when Ryan says he's sorry he's got his toys everywhere, but he doesn't mean it, because he keeps doing it again.)

Then finally Hitler invaded Poland and the Allies had to say, "Enough's enough," call his bluff and have a war. A bit like when my mum tells Ryan if he hasn't stopped shouting by the time she's counted to three, he will be sent to his room. Then, after three, my mum *has* to send Ryan to his room otherwise he will become an out-of-control tyrant. (Well, it's a *bit* like that. I'm not saying my little brother is like Hitler.)

Anyway, a cartoon about Hitler is quite serious. Maybe Tammy means more like Gary Larson? I have a look through my Gary Larson book. (I *love* my Gary

147

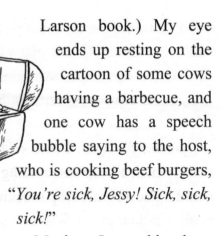

Larson book.) My eye ends up resting on the cartoon of some cows having a barbecue, and one cow has a speech bubble saying to the host, who is cooking beef burgers, *"You're sick, Jessy! Sick, sick, sick!"*

Maybe I could draw Amelia as a cow having a barbecue but dressed like Hitler? Um. *Hmm*. I feel a bit out of my depth. Maybe I can't do this. Let's have a think.

What is Amelia like? She's vain, superficial, shallow, snobby and insulting. And cliquey and obsessed with fashion and rude to people she thinks are beneath her. And y'know, why does it matter if my jacket came from *Primark*? Who gets to decide what's rubbish, anyway? I don't see how having more money makes you a better person.

So Amelia has completely the wrong priorities. But how exactly can I mock that? I mean, I suppose I could try to exaggerate them for comic effect. I mean, it *is* like she thinks the "right" clothes are more

148

important than caring about people. She'd probably exclude Mother Teresa and Gandhi because their clothes weren't expensive enough. Maybe I could draw that? Um, no. OK, let's have a bit more of a think about this.

I ponder for ages. Loads of ideas float round my head, which I keep discounting as I think. Maybe I could make a comic strip mocking Amelia's gang for being shallow but it'd be better as just one picture. I think about drawing a cartoon of Amelia as a weasel making fun of a stoat who isn't wearing a cool enough jacket, but it just doesn't seem powerful enough, somehow.

Think, Jessica, *think*. What does Amelia care about? Well, fashion. What would upset her? Apart from having to shop at the same shops as me.

Then I have a brainwave and I remember how mean some fashion magazines can be. Like sometimes they have a picture of a famous actress on the red carpet or something, and they put a tick or a cross by her outfit, like the outfit was homework and she's done it all wrong. (When, really, no one asked for the magazine's opinion and the actress might really like her dress.)

Or there's that "Circle of Shame" thing where a magazine has photos of celebrities showing sweat patches under their arms or wrinkles under their chins, and they mock them for not being well groomed enough. (Even though everybody sweats and has wrinkles, and that's *normal*.)

That is the sort of thing that would upset Amelia. That would probably be her worst nightmare. But I can't just do that, or it's like I agree that fashion is important. I will have to turn it on its head and do a *parody* ...

Yeah! Then I can mock the mean things about fashion *and* Amelia all at the same time. Brilliant. I've decided. I am going to draw Amelia as "The Hellfern Juniors' Fashion-Victim Sheep". It's a bit of a long-winded title, but I figure I should build on the earlier success of the Hellfern brand. Plus, that makes it more relevant to everyone.

I draw a vain-looking cartoon sheep standing on its hind legs wearing sunglasses. It has a comedy hat with a slogan on it saying "Richer than U" and it's wearing a small CAC badge pinned to its T-shirt.

I draw the circle-of-shame circle and a line coming

off the sheep. But instead of a sweat patch, I make it about something Amelia should *actually* be ashamed of, like making my best friend gang up on me. So in the circle I do a close-up of one of the front hooves holding a white envelope, and put, "OMG! Shameful! Plays nasty tricks on people" as the highlighted crime.

Then I do the "what's-she-wearing" lines coming off the cartoon sheep, and start drawing some ridiculous clothes. My favourite is what I do with the shoes. I give the sheep's back hooves "reverse high heels", and put in the box coming off it: "Latest fashion to make you look shorter. Sounds silly, and v. hard to walk in, but a top magazine said they were good, so they must be."

I make the T-shirt the Amelia-sheep is wearing an MBlaze band T-shirt, with tiny cartoon men on it. It's a lot like a real fan T-shirt, except their slogan says, "MBlaze – no. 1 for crying about drivel".

Then I draw a couple more badges pinned to the T-shirt saying, "Down with individual thoughts"

and, "Everyone who doesn't want to be exactly like me should be bullied."

I wanted to add a McDonald's-style name tag saying, "Hello, my name is Amelia and I'm here to insult you," but there wasn't enough room in the end.

There. I think I might be done. I sit back and admire my handiwork. I'm quite proud of it, actually. I study my cartoon, and giggle slightly at how funny and daring I have been.

To be honest, I feel quite a lot better. I feel like a weight has been lifted somehow. I think by doing this I must have vented all my frustrations. Now I feel light and happy. And I think Amelia is an idiot. Ha ha – she's a sheep!

I mean, there is no way I could actually hand this out in school, though. Masses undermining The Man or no masses undermining The Man. I've gone way too far for that. It's really quite offensive. I giggle again. Yeah, there's no way I'm giving this out. Then I'd be as bad as she is.

Plus, I quite like this being my own little secret. And I can just look at this picture to cheer myself up whenever Amelia makes me feel blue. I'm a *genius*. I admire it some more and then put it in my

school bag. This cartoon is going to be
my "Amelia Stress-Buster!"

CHAPTER 15

I'm still feeling pretty Zen and pleased with myself as I ride the bus to school the next day. I have my stress-busting cartoon in my bag, which my sister said *definitely* did qualify as a satirical cartoon. How good is that?

Tammy also said she really liked it and that I should definitely show it to everyone at school. Right before she got chucked out of my room by my parents so that she couldn't "pollute" my or Ryan's "young minds" against the dangers of capitalism any more. (Little did they know she was *actually* trying to convince me to start a vendetta against a new girl at school – which I think might be worse than capitalism, in some ways.)

Anyway, I'm still not going to hand it out. Tammy is way too into conflict and really doesn't seem to be able to tell (or care) when doing something will make the situation worse. This cartoon is just for me. Well, I might show it to Joshua; he'd probably like it. And maybe Tanya, but that's *it*.

Mind you, I'm surprised my parents don't support my sister's views a bit more. I mean, the fact we're still on an economy drive kind of suggests that capitalism hasn't worked out that well for us. But some people just can't be told. Or convinced to get a dog.

I can see why my parents are annoyed with Tammy, though. I do get that she has kind of used my and Ryan's "young minds" (and love of animals) to try and make my parents do something they don't want to. *But*, the point is – it's *for a good cause*. (Just like my dastardly cartoon-scheme.) Plus, we'd get a dog. And dogs are awesome.

Natalie and Amelia look up as I enter 6C, and stop talking. I ignore them as best I can, trying not to feel nervous, and go over to my desk anyway.

"Oh, look who it is," says Amelia to me. "The mystery litter lout."

"What?" I say, taken aback.

"Bit cowardly, isn't it? Hiding behind a bit of paper. Thought you liked to stand on your own two feet," she continues.

Oh God, how does she know? She *can't* have seen my cartoon. For one thing it's still in my bag and no one at school has seen it. I nervously stroke my bag with one hand. She can't know; has she *guessed*? No way! If Amelia has the powers of the thought police, that would really be the *living end*.

"I don't know what you're talking about," I say truthfully.

"All right, play it that way," says Amelia coolly. "But we might just have a little *surprise* of our own. Actually, do you know how to *spell* that?" She smirks.

"T-h-a-t," I joke before I can stop myself. *What's wrong with me?* Part of me is a little bit scared of what on earth horrible Amelia is talking about now, and here I am making silly jokes!

Amelia gives me a disgusted look and then raises her desk lid so she doesn't have to look at me. She and Natalie start whispering. Well, I don't care. (I do care a bit.) But *officially*, I don't care. And what's spelling got to do with it, anyway?

OK. So I know what spelling has to do with it now. There is a notice in assembly about the inter-form spelling bee championship. Anyone interested is supposed to sign up. And *get this* – Amelia has signed me up! I'm so rubbish at spelling, I will definitely lose. She obviously wants to see me humiliated. Honestly. If this isn't the *living end*, it must be close to it.

I'm determined to un-sign myself. At break time I decide to head to the staffroom to tell Mrs Cole, our form teacher, that I'm not doing the spelling bee and to take me off the list. Huh, maybe I *should* photocopy my cartoon. No, no way. I would never do that. Why *has* Amelia entered me in the spelling bee, though?

"Toons! Oi, Toons! Slow down!" It's Tanya Harris. I stop attempting to push my way through the throng of people heading for the canteen and turn back to meet her. Tanya would *love* my cartoon sheep. And I'm so angry with Amelia I want her to see it.

"Hey, Tanya, look at this," I say, pulling the

cartoon out of my bag as soon as she reaches me. Tanya surveys the "Hellfern Juniors' Fashion-Victim Sheep" with interest and then snorts delighted laughter.

"Oh, Toons, this is *brilliant*. You did this? You should have said. I wouldn't have already taken care of things for you." A warning bell goes off in my head.

"Oh, um … what, Tanya?"

"Like I said, I took care of things for you. I got your back, remember? 'Cause we're in a gang and that. I said I'd be your muscle. Sorted."

"What did you do?" I try not to sound panicked.

"Shantair told me they played a trick on you with some letter. She saw the whole thing. Well out of order. Nasty cows. We can't have that. Not little Toons. You're too nice. That's like picking on Bambi or something. So I printed this out in free computer time, during IT." She hands me a folded-up piece of paper.

"Just a little warning shot across the bows. Something to make them think twice before doing anything like that again. I put one of these on Amelia's desk this morning."

"Oh wow, did you?" I'm momentarily speechless.

I unfold the piece of paper. In massive capital letters, in black computer print, it says,

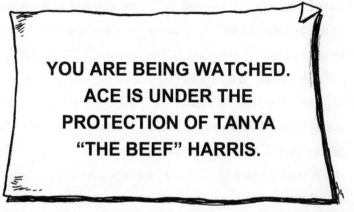

**YOU ARE BEING WATCHED.
ACE IS UNDER THE
PROTECTION OF TANYA
"THE BEEF" HARRIS.**

Oh. My. Goodness. It's like some kind of Mafia warning. OK, part of me is amused and kind of impressed that Tanya has managed to use free computer time in IT to print out threats. It's sort of enterprising, in a way. But *still*.

"You're welcome." Tanya beams. Then she winks and saunters off down the now less crowded corridor.

I head towards the staffroom feeling flustered. I can't decide if I'm more pleased or more terrified that I'm under Tanya's "protection" and she wrote that note. I think in a way I'm flattered. Though also embarrassed at having to be "rescued". I've never been sure where I fitted in at school, but now I know: I am the equivalent of Bambi – to Tanya Harris.

And now I also know what Amelia was talking about this morning, and why she entered me in the spelling bee in the first place. Plus, Amelia clearly thinks I *asked* Tanya to put ACE under her protection. Which I didn't. (So in a way Tanya has caused this stupid spelling problem.)

To my utter dismay, Mrs Cole won't let me un-sign myself from the spelling bee. She's in a hurry when I catch her at the end of break, and in no mood to negotiate.

"But what if I told you I didn't even enter? Someone played a trick on me," I say.

"Look, Jessica, I don't know what you're talking about, but this is no time for silly indecisiveness. There's no way you're un-signing yourself. This will be great for you."

"Oh." I consider the bind I appear to be in. "But it won't. Honestly, Mrs Cole. I'm rubbish at spelling. It's going to be embarrassing. Please let me un-sign, *please*."

"Now, listen here, Jessica," says Mrs Cole, sounding serious. "You are a perfectly clever girl, and there is no reason in the world that you won't improve at spelling if you just put the work in. Trying is a brilliant thing, you know. It gets you many places." (I can't think of *anywhere* good that trying has got me at the moment.) "Plus, there are cash prizes."

"Cash prizes?"

"Well, iTunes vouchers. But that's as good as cash, isn't it? I'm sure that's what you young things would spend your money on anyway."

"Well …"

"And on an unrelated matter, your art teacher, Mrs Cooper, tells me you are very good at drawing."

"I, um …"

"So I very much hope that you will enter the Easter bonnet drawing competition as well."

"Well, that sounds very nice but—"

"Get *involved*, Jessica. The spelling bee should be fun. Come on, what have you got to lose?" (*Hello?* Only my dignity, or what remains of it.)

"Mrs Cole, please—"

"No, Jessica. You're doing it. Break's over now, I

believe you have a class to get to? Now *that* would be embarrassing, if you were *late*."

And then she brushes past me, off to the next lesson. I am *stuck* in the spelling bee. I *hate* Amelia.

A weird thing happens at the end of the day.

"Are you going to swot up on your spellings before tomorrow?" asks Cherry as we start heading towards chess club. "Because I definitely think you should." (This isn't the weird thing, btw – we always go to chess club on a Wednesday, and Cherry is always telling me to study more.)

"I'm not sure it would make that much difference," I reply.

"I really think you should at least *try*, though," says Cherry.

"Um. Well, the thing is, it's just a—"

"Hey, nice cartoon!" says a boy called Luke as he passes us in the corridor.

"Really funny sheep," adds his friend, Sam. Then they're gone.

That's the weird thing.

For a second I think: that's odd. Why would

anyone congratulate me on … Then I think: NO WAY! Nooooo!

"What are they talking about?" asks Cherry as I suddenly scrabble through my bag, trying to find my stress-busting picture. It's not in there!

"Oh no," I whisper.

"What?"

"I think … Cherry, I think Tanya Harris *might* have taken a cartoon I drew of – well, kind of – of Amelia, and photocopied it."

Oh *God*, how could I have not *noticed* she took it? I was so flustered. Tanya probably photocopied it thinking she was doing me a *favour*! I never got round to explaining the whole private, *stress-busting* nature of the cartoon, I was too distracted by her scary note.

Well, it's not *decisively* Amelia. It doesn't have her name on it. *Thank God*. I cringe as I remember how I nearly added that. *Ohhh*. Why did I show it to Tanya? Why?

OK, focus. It's just a funny cartoon. It's just a funny sheep cartoon, mocking a certain type of person (which Amelia happens to be) but it is not *aimed* at her.

Ohhh. I didn't do this. Tanya did this. (I kind of did this.) But it's Tanya's fault, not mine. Maybe if I find Tanya, I can find out how many copies she made, and stop them getting any further. Yeah. Maybe Amelia won't even see it.

"*There* you are!" A shout comes from behind us. We turn around. Amelia is standing there, looking livid. Natalie is a little bit behind her. I'm going to go out on a limb here and say I think Amelia *might* have already seen the "Hellfern Juniors' Fashion-Victim Sheep" cartoon.

"Hi there," I say, weirdly amicable.

"Drawn anything lately?" sneers Amelia.

"Hey," I say. "Firstly, I did not photocopy that. And secondly, prove it."

Amelia carries on. "What makes you such an expert on how to be nice to people, anyway?" She kind of sounds upset. I suppose you would be. Even if you were Amelia.

"Amelia, let's just go," says Natalie.

"Fine," says Amelia. "But don't think I don't know that sheep is meant to be me!"

"Look, it's actually a complete accident," I explain. "I never meant anyone to see it."

Amelia glares at me disbelievingly, with a slightly insane expression on her face. "I am going to *ANNIHILATE* you in the spelling bee tomorrow!" she yells.

If I'm completely honest, I have mixed feelings about all this. Amelia has been really mean to me and part of me is glad she's annoyed. But the rest of me feels a bit sorry for her. I never meant to gang up on her. And she *is* new.

"I don't care about the stupid spelling bee," I say. "I only care that you've taken my best friend away and been really horrible to me. I didn't mean for that cartoon to get out but, *whatever*, Amelia. What goes around comes around."

Natalie and Amelia stare at me, open-mouthed. Cherry and I turn our backs on them and go to chess club.

CHAPTER 16

Well, I didn't expect this turn of events. I didn't expect to blurt out the truth about how I feel to Natalie and Amelia while a cartoon I drew but didn't intend to distribute is doing the rounds.

Honestly, though, I'm a little bit confused. I've been trying to get Amelia back for ages. Now I've sort of done it, it doesn't actually feel that good. It feels mean. *I didn't do it*, I remind myself. I wash my hands of this. I really do. Well, I really would if I just didn't feel quite so guilty.

Amelia is horrible. In many ways she had it coming. I'm over it. I'm over this whole Amelia thing. Except …

I think it's just that I've successfully upset

I hate spelling!

and annoyed Amelia so much that she's actually threatened me with *annihilation*. At a spelling bee. I mean, I'm not able to take either of those things seriously but the point is, she lost her cool.

I think for the first time I can see her as this tiny new girl, trying to fit in. Desperately trying to do anything she can to make and keep new friends. (Even if it means victimising their existing friends.) She's been constantly trying to act cool and popular so that people will like her.

But now she's lost her cool and, in my eyes at least, she's lost her power. So Tammy was right about the power of a satirical cartoon. I'm not scared of her any more. I just feel a bit sorry for her. That won't stop her, of course, and she is going to gloat a lot about this spelling bee. God, I hate spelling.

So, I probably should be practising my spelling now. But what I'm actually doing is using the family laptop to look at videos of people falling over. I really should stop in a minute and do some work. Well, just one more.

My sister is still here. I think she's been out on some kind of march or protest or something about cuts to public services. There was another fight

167

between her and my parents. Now she's gone out again, but I think she's coming back tonight.

It's a shame she's out, because she could help test me on spellings. Ryan doesn't understand enough long words to help me. And I don't want to ask my parents because then they'll know I'm in a spelling bee and they'll make me do loads of work, as if it's actually important or something.

But, you know, it's actually all Tammy's fault that I am still watching videos on the computer instead of learning how to spell. I am definitely going to stop in a minute. Just one more.

So it's Thursday. The spelling bee is at lunchtime and I've done nothing. Well, not *nothing*. I tested myself to see if I could spell disestablishmentarianism. And I couldn't. Also, I don't know what it means. But that's a really long word, isn't it? That's bound not to come up.

I don't know what I was thinking. I should have been testing myself on more likely words like "investigate" and "remember". If only I'd remembered. Ha ha, I am funny. Even in times of crisis. Oh *God*.

I sign up for the Easter bonnet competition at break time, on the way to art. I figure I might as well. I'm sure this is exactly the sort of thing that Amelia would say makes me babyish, but I don't care, I like drawing.

According to the jovial-looking notice, we just have to draw what we think a brilliant Easter bonnet would look like. 6C and 6P are going head to head, just like in the spelling bee.

I love how our school tries to make it sound exciting, like it's wrestling or something. "*Two* will enter, only *one* will leave." (OK, they don't exactly do that, but they might as well.) It's daft if you ask me.

Hmm. The notice says the best ones will be displayed, and the winners will get Easter eggs. *Easter eggs?* What happened to *cash prizes*? (Or iTunes vouchers?) Don't get me wrong, I LOVE chocolate. But it's almost as if they are saying that drawing shouldn't be taken as seriously as spelling, or something.

"Hey, how come you're entering

169

the Easter bonnet competition?" asks Joshua, arriving at my side.

"Why not?"

"Bit beneath your talents, isn't it?" he says. I chuckle. At least he didn't say it was babyish.

"Well, there aren't that many competitions that reward drawing. I thought I might as well," I say.

"Don't waste your time with this," he continues. "I've got a better idea. I was going to talk to you about it in art."

I briefly ignore Joshua and finish signing my name. I don't care what he says, I'm still entering this competition.

"Right," I say as we walk towards the art room. "I'm all ears."

It turns out Joshua wants to start some kind of regular fanzine or comic thing with me. Blimey!

"And each issue could have a new caricature," he says.

"Caricature?" I look puzzled.

"Yes, caricature," he grins. "You do know what a caricature is, don't you?"

Um ... "God yes, I'm not an idiot," I say hotly. OK, so I *think* a caricature is a cheeky cartoon making fun of someone's appearance. Like when people exaggerate how big Prince Charles's ears really are.

"Good, 'cause that one you did about snobby girls in our year being fashion victims was really funny."

Ha! I'm right! And I've already done one. My fashion-victim sheep is a *caricature*. Who knew? Bloody Joshua, thinks he knows everything. And he's *still* talking …

"We could do that to all the other groups. You know, you could draw funny pictures of the sporty people and the nerdy people and that. Could be a series. Could be, like, our last year of Hillfern Juniors *legacy*."

Blimey! On the one hand – what an exciting idea! But on the other hand – really? Would there really be a demand for that?

"And we could do other comic strips and stuff," he continues. "I've got some mates that would love to do those. And we could do funny articles, and news about the school, but the real stuff, not the fluffy stuff."

"Oh, yes," I say, nodding.

"And then we could *charge* for it," says Joshua with a flourish. This seems to be the end of his speech. We take our seats at our table. "What do you think?" He looks at me.

I'm not sure what to say. I'm just not sure. I suppose really I'm scared that we'll go to all that trouble and no one will want it.

"Um. It kind of *sounds* like a really cool idea …" I trail off.

"Is there an *and* or a *but* coming?" asks Joshua.

"Well," I say.

"Or a *well*?" he asks without missing a beat. I can't help but laugh.

I suppose really it would be fun to spend more time with him. And I love drawing and making stuff. And this would be a brilliant way to do all those things. And whoever gained anything by not taking chances?

I mean, just yesterday Mrs Cole was telling me to do more trying. Or something. So in many ways, making a cartoon comic strip mocking the school would be *obeying my teacher's orders* …

Oh, you know what? I think too much.

"I'm in," I say, grinning.

"Brilliant," says Joshua. "Now we just need a name."

Oh no, not the name thing again. It took me *ages* to think of ACE. Here we go again … But apart from that, this is blimmin' brilliant.

So what would you say if I told you a miracle happened at the spelling bee, and I won? That's right, that I was lying.

Of course there was no miracle. I didn't put the work in and I'm terrible at spelling. *C'est la vie.* (That's French for *such is life*. It's a shame it wasn't a French test, really. I'm better at that.)

Anyway, the silver lining is that Amelia didn't win, either. She came second. I appreciate that this is a small, *pyrrhic* victory. (That means empty and hollow victory – can you *believe* that came up as a word we had to spell? I had no chance. But on the plus side – I learned a new word.)

I sort of found the spelling bee funny in the end. I couldn't help it. I think partly I feel quite excited about doing cartoons with Joshua, so other stuff that used to scare me just doesn't faze me at the moment.

And I'm off the hook about the sheep cartoon. Not one person thought it was of Amelia, apart from Amelia. She's had absolutely no hassle at all. People just think it's a joke about a type of person. A *caricature*.

Plus, I got more answers right in the spelling bee than I thought I would (I remembered how to spell *remember* – result). Then I messed up (seriously – *pyrrhic* – come *on*). And Amelia did quite a lot of gloating.

But I don't care. (OK, I *mainly* don't care.) Spelling is just not where my skill set lies. We can't all be good at everything. And the world would be boring if we were all the same. And it's not my fault that the things I am bad at are considered more important by the world than the things I am good at. It's just one step away from fascism to say otherwise. (Maybe I've been hanging around my sister too long?)

Anyway, the point is, this spelling nonsense is over now and I can move on with my life.

An even weirder thing happens at the end of the day than the weird thing that happened at the end of yesterday. As the bell goes in our form, and we're all about to stampede out in our coats, Amelia comes up to me.

"I want to talk to you," she says.

Oh God, I think. I bet she's prepared a really vicious speech to shout at me for drawing that cartoon. It probably contains loads of jokes about how I can't spell, and am illiterate and stupid or something …

"Um. Do you?" I manage, as our classmates file past us. Apart from Natalie, who stands just behind Amelia.

"Yeah," says Amelia. "I … um … I think we should be, um … *friends*."

Nothing had prepared me for this turn of events. (What fresh trickery is *this*?)

"What?" I say.

"Look, it can't have been easy for you today when I beat you in the spelling bee," begins Amelia. (Actually, it was surprisingly easy.) "But you took it really well. And, well, I just wanted to say, in some ways, it … seems like a shame that we're fighting."

What the what? *What?* Seriously. OK, either this

175

is a new trick or I am hearing things. "What are you saying?" I ask Amelia. (I mean, not actually *sorry* by the sounds of things, but what on earth is going on?)

"I'm trying to say," falters Amelia, "that we—"

"Look, you know what," I interrupt tiredly. "I'm really not in the mood for more tricks. I'm sure whatever you had planned is hilarious, but I'm bored of you now." I go to start moving.

"No!" says Amelia. "It's not a trick this time. Look, I think things have got a bit silly between us, competing in the way we have …"

(*Competing?* To see who's got the meanest streak? Not a very close competition, that. You win hands down, I think.)

"… And I know I've been just as bad as you …"

(No, *worse*, Amelia, you've been much *worse* than me. And *you started it*, I think.)

"… But it's silly to keep going against each other in little competitions, like the spelling bee. Which I won. And I just wanted to say, it's … it's a silly competition … And I've won, and …" (Blimey, could she get the fact that she won into that sentence any more? Especially as *actually*, she came second.)

Amelia is struggling for words. "Um … And we

should … *be* … *friends*," she finishes finally. But she says the last two words much more quietly, as if she's uncomfortable saying them. It's a struggle to hear them.

"Pardon?" I say.

"We should be friends." Amelia says it again, much louder this time, and with a touch of annoyance in her voice. She glances at Natalie.

Now, I'm no detective, but if I had to hazard a guess here, I would say that Natalie has put Amelia up to this. I don't think Amelia has had a change of heart, or really wants to be my friend at all. This is odd.

On the surface, it looks a bit like Amelia is trying to *quit while she's ahead*. Like she feels like she's *beaten* me, and wants our feud to end *on her terms*. Or maybe because she's sick of Tanya Harris attempting to trip her up in the corridor all the time.

But actually, from her body language, and occasional glances at Natalie (who looks kind of nervous) I'd say that Amelia may very well still hate me and that she is doing this for Natalie.

Which means that (a) Natalie has finally stuck up for me; and (b) Amelia must really like Natalie, if she's prepared to be nice to me (who she doesn't like) for Natalie's sake.

Hmm. I'm really not sure what to do. Is it a good idea for two people who clearly hate each other to lie and say they don't hate each other, that they in fact like each other, for the greater good of their other friend?

"Um, so you want to be friends?" I say finally.

"That's what I said, isn't it?" snaps Amelia, who then recovers herself and adds, "Because I do."

Hmmm. I'm really not sure I can see this working. I mean, for one thing, I'm not sure Amelia will be able to go an hour without calling me stupid and unfashionable. But on the other hand, Natalie clearly wants to be friends again. *Hmmm.*

"Um, Amelia, that's really *nice,*" I lie. (It isn't nice and you don't mean it, I add silently.) "Let's try and be nice to each other and see how that goes." I mean, *that's* at least honest. *Saying* you're friends doesn't mean anything. It's how you *behave* that counts.

"Brilliant," says Amelia, holding out her hand. We shake.

"Oh, I'm so glad you two have finally put this behind you," says Natalie, coming forward.

(Honestly, sometimes I wonder about Natalie's perception of the world.)

"Jess, I'm so sorry about that trick we played about the bowling," she continues. "I've been feeling *awful* about it. It might be the worst thing I've ever done. It's just, I was so hurt. That day I rang you, I really felt I'd gone out on a limb, and it was really hard to say all that stuff, and I *so* thought we were going to be friends again, and then you rejected me and hung up. I was devastated. But it made me really angry. I know it's no excuse. We didn't even go bowling."

"Yeah, I'm sorry about that, too," says Amelia.

"Thanks," I say. (I *suppose* I should apologise as well.) "Er, I'm sorry about that sheep cartoon, by the way. But honestly, no one was meant to see it. Tanya Harris photocopied it without my permission."

"That's OK, no harm done," replies Natalie, though Amelia doesn't say anything. "Come on, let's get the bus," says Natalie. We all walk out together. It's all gone a bit formal and weird.

"Oh yeah, so Amelia had this idea," says Natalie, when we reach the bus stop.

"Yeah, I was thinking," says Amelia. "If ever you want to make any more cartoons for badges, we

can put them through
Cassy's badgemaker.
If you want."

"Isn't that a nice idea?"
says Natalie brightly.

"Er, yeah, cool," I say.
I mean, I *suppose* it's
cool. They probably think
they're being really nice to me,
and including me or something.

But what they don't realise is that now I'm a
famous cartoonist (to upwards of fifty people) and
have been invited to have my work *published* (in a
homemade fanzine), I'm just a lot harder to impress.
But fame hasn't changed me. Ha ha. *Hmmmmm.*

CHAPTER 17

I still can't believe I'm sort of *friends* with Natalie again. I mean, I *am*. I *am* friends with her. It doesn't quite feel real. Well, I've *said* I'm friends with her again. I don't completely *feel* like I am, though. But I am. We are friends.

I'm kind of weirdly bamboozled as I reach my house and I don't notice the VanDerks in their front garden, chatting to my mum over the fence again.

This time the VanDerks have been boasting that their kid, Harriet, won the Year Six spelling bee. She's the one who beat Amelia. Predictably this has awakened my mum's competitive streak and she is annoyed that I didn't even mention that I was entering. (Blimmin' Harriet – what's she telling everyone *I* entered for?)

"I wish you'd mentioned you were doing it," says my mum. "We could have helped you last night. And then you might have won!"

"Mum, I think we should stick to reality," I say. "I would never have won a spelling bee."

"That's not the attitude to have," says my mum. (*Honestly*, I could really do without this.) I've got important things to do, like worry if I am really friends with Natalie again.

"Your mum's right," says Mr VanDerk unhelpfully. "You have to think like a winner if you want to be a winner." *I'm not on trial here.* Why can't they drop it? Just 'cause their stupid kid won.

"Well, it's all in the past now," I say dismissively, trying to sweep this conversation aside. "And it's only a spelling bee."

"There's no such thing as *only*," says Mr VanDerk. "An achievement is an achievement, whatever it is. It's always something to be proud of."

Yeah, yeah, I think. I end up agreeing with him out of politeness and we say goodbye soon after that. My mum continues to make references to how I should try harder as we go inside.

I think there's a real danger that my mum has had her head turned by the VanDerks' weird, over-achieving children, and that it's coloured her vision of what's *normal*. I mean, I *am* actually really hard-working compared to loads of the kids at my school. (I bet if I introduced her to Tanya Harris she'd appreciate how academic I really am.)

When we get inside, we find my sister has really upped her game in the "how to convince my parents to get a rescue dog" stakes. And this time it's almost theatrical.

As my mum and I enter the kitchen, we see a pile of freshly bought groceries, including salad, cheese and fajita sauce. On top of it is a note and a picture of a really cute dog, its big sad eyes looking straight at the camera.

The note says:

> Dear Morris Family,
>
> Please accept this gift of fajita ingredients as a token of my appreciation of what I hope you will do for me in the future. I know you have been on an economy drive, but I want you to know I would be no trouble at all, and I already love you as if you were my own. Yours sincerely, Fido.
>
> PS. I would totally protect the house and I could be trained to bark at the VanDerks.

I think this is quite funny, but I'm not sure my mum does. "Your sister is an absolute nutjob," she states.

So what has two thumbs and the most delicious fajitas dinner ever? *This guy*. (You can't see me but … my thumbs … yadda yadda – you know the drill.) I wish my sister would try to convince my parents to do stuff through the medium of food more often.

I feel quietly happy as I sit in my room later that night, drawing and shading in my Easter bonnet for

184

the competition. I've decided to use one of my last really big bits of paper from the giant pad that I got for Christmas.

I draw quite a traditional-looking bonnet near the bottom of the page, with a blue ribbon tied in a bow. Then on top of the bonnet, I draw loads and loads of piled-up fruit. There's pineapples, bananas, grapes, oranges – basically all the fruit I can think of. It goes up like a pyramid, and on the top of the very peak is a strawberry.

I use my felt tips this time, so it looks really vibrant and colourful. I think it's quite eye-catching. It takes ages. My hand is starting to hurt towards the end, from all the shading. But I think it's worth it. I'm quite pleased with it.

Every now and then Joshua texts me a funny message, and I text one back. I told him I am drawing loads of fruit, and he said he'd heard Mr Scot (one of the teachers judging the competition) was a fan of "big melons" so I was in with a good chance. Sometimes he's very rude. He almost makes me look polite! But he *is* funny. I like him a lot.

When I've finished, I try and tidy my desk a bit and knock some paper on to the floor. When I pick it up I realise that one of the bits of paper is an MBlaze poem that Natalie and I wrote together. It reads:

Oh Ricky, Chesney, Baz and Dave
We've got advice that you
should save
We don't know why you sing of
dating
When all your girlfriends sound
like Satan
No one gets a Nobel Prize
For smashing chemistry sets
before our eyes
We don't know why you sing of failing
And have people reward your
constant wailing
If you're not good with women
you should move on
And stop singing such boring songs
We don't know how you have careers
We really can't believe our ears
So maybe take some time out
rest in bed
And give other musicians
a chance instead

I giggle as I read it, remembering how much fun we had writing this. Natalie kept making some of the words rude and we had to keep scribbling them out in case our parents saw it.

On the back of the piece of paper, it says,

"Dear Jessica, keep this poem to remember the day we wrote M Blaze poems XXXXXXXX" Then at the bottom it says, "N&J Best Friends Forever. If Destroyed Still True."

I feel kind of choked up as I read it. I'm transported back to the day we wrote this, and how close we were, and how much fun it was. I realise there is *no way* I'm not going to be proper friends with Natalie again. I've missed her too much. Everything is going to be brilliant. We can make this work.

Ryan comes in just as I am putting the poem away carefully in my desk drawer, wanting to play Lego pirates again. He seems quite impressed with my bonnet picture, saying, "It makes fruit look much nicer than it really is."

I figure I just about have time to play – I mean *help*, nah, *play* – Lego pirates with Ryan, so he goes and gets his stuff (and Winnie the Pooh for good measure) and brings it all into my room.

"Right," says Ryan, once he's happy with where he's set up the ship. "A lot has happened since last time, so I'd better fill you in."

He isn't kidding. There is a whole world in Ryan's head. It's actually kind of amazing. I mean, to be fair, *a lot* of it is quite heavily plagiarised from loads of films he has seen. (I don't really see why pirates would be interested in trying to find the Arc of the Covenant.) But still.

I'm actually kind of confused, though. "Hang on, Ryan," I say, pointing to a little stripy-topped Lego man, the first mate who rebelled and formed a rival gang in our last game. "I thought Jimmy was—"

"That's not Jimmy," interrupts Ryan.

"What? Yes, it is."

"No. We've started again with a new story," says Ryan. "That's Herman now."

"*Herman?*" I repeat. Seriously. "I can't keep up with these changes, Ryan. Make your mind up."

"No," says Ryan, looking a bit affronted. "We did the other story. It finished. When it's too long, it gets boring and you have to have a new adventure."

Well, all right, maybe he has a point about that. Things do get boring when they go on too long. I mean, look at double geography. (*Ha ha*, I just mentally high-fived myself for that one.)

Actually, now I come to think of it, that's kind of what I've just done, let go of a long boring story so I can be proper friends with Natalie again. And actually it was Ryan's Lego pirates that gave me the idea for the gang in the first place.

Is this really going to be a metaphor for my life? A six-year-old's thoughts on Lego men? Because just *once* I would like to learn a life lesson from something that *wasn't* pirate Lego.

CHAPTER 18

Yay! It's Friday – the best day of the week. And I am going to go into school with a *clean slate*, like my brother's Lego pirates. Kind of. I mean, I'll fire fewer cannon, obviously, but you get the idea.

And I am going to be positive. I'm looking *forward* to school. How weird is that? I am going to hand in my *ace* Easter bonnet drawing, chat to my new friend Joshua, and be friends properly with Natalie again. And if bad things happen, so what? There will be some good things coming along again eventually. That is the way it works.

In the form room before registration Natalie asks to have a *quick word* with me. Curious, I follow her out into the corridor and we go round the corner, under some stairs where our coats are hung on pegs.

"Jessica, I wanted to say sorry properly," she says. "So I got you this."

She's got me a present! "You didn't need to do that!" I beam, tearing into the pretty pink and silver paper, and revealing a small jewellery box. (I didn't get her anything – but then she has been meaner to me than I have to her.) Inside the box is a silver necklace with a pendant in the shape of one half of a broken heart.

"Look, I have the other half," says Natalie, pulling it out from under her shirt collar. "If you put them together the heart becomes whole again and they say 'Best Friends Forever'. That way we're best friends, even when we're not together." She holds her broken heart against mine, and the zigzag line matches up perfectly.

"Oh, *wow*!" I gasp. "I don't know what to say! Natalie, I love it!"

I have this feeling I might be about to cry. That would be silly. This is a happy occasion.

Natalie fastens the necklace around my

neck for me and I blink hard. I *love* this necklace.

Natalie steps back and surveys it. "Oh, don't! You'll set me off!" she says, clocking my tears. Her eyes are red, too, and we both laugh and wipe at our eyes with our hands. "Oh, Jess, I am *so sorry*! Let's never fight like that again!" she exclaims, and flings her arms around me.

I really feel like we've resolved something, and I feel close to Natalie again. I feel like I could tell her anything, any secret, and she is my best friend, and she will understand me (even when I am weird). All the bad stuff really has gone now. I mean, surely if we can come through *that*, we can come through anything.

Also, this necklace is only for *two* people. So Amelia *can't* have one, and I am definitely Natalie's best, number one friend. Not that that matters or anything – I mean, I am being very positive about everything, anyway. I'm just saying, is all.

We pull apart and joke about how we are idiots for crying. Finally we manage to control ourselves and go back into the form room for registration.

I gave in my Easter bonnet picture for the competition. It's up on the display wall with all the others, and, well, it kind of stands out. It didn't even occur to me that most people would (a) do it on some A4-sized paper. (Mine is huge.) And (b) that most people would literally just draw a simple, brown bonnet. (Mine is very colourful. And covered in fruit.)

Hmmm. I mean, a couple of people have done more creative pictures, with rabbit ears and stuff, but basically, mine stands out a *mile* away. I can't work out if that is a good or a bad thing.

Joshua, Natalie and Amelia all come with me to the lunchtime announcement of the winner and runners-up. Amelia is really trying to be nice to me.

"Which one is yours?" she asks.

"The fruit one."

"Blimey, it's a bit camp, isn't it?" she comments. (All right, she's *kind of* trying to be nice to me.)

The teachers start announcing the runners-up. Harriet VanDerk is a runner-up. *Typical.* And her bonnet was really *boring*. She hadn't added anything inventive to it *at all*.

"And now for the winner," Mr Scot is saying at the front of the hall. (Natalie squeezes my hand.) Mr Scot chuckles. "Well, it couldn't really be anyone else, could it? Jessica Morris! What a lot of fruit! Come up here and receive your Easter egg."

I've won! I've *won*! I've beaten all of 6P as well as 6C! I've beaten Harriet VanDerk at something! Oh my goodness! I go up and receive my giant Easter egg while everyone claps. I don't think I've ever *won* anything before.

So this is what victory feels like! I've always wondered. It's quite good, I suppose. People keep congratulating me (and asking to share my Easter egg). I can sort of see why people go on about winning now.

"See, I told you, it's all about the melons," jokes Joshua, patting me on the shoulder.

"It's a shame it wasn't a

194

better prize, like money and stuff," says Amelia.

"Yeah," agrees Harriet VanDerk, coming over. "I suppose they're getting you used to the idea that cartoonists are never going to be rich." She chuckles.

"Yeah," says Joshua sarcastically. "I think that's how Matt Groening paid for his house, with Easter eggs."

"Well done on being a runner-up, Harriet," I say politely.

"Yeah, thanks," says Harriet. (She doesn't return the compliment.) "I have to say, I think you cheated slightly," she adds.

"What?" I'm shocked.

"Well, a great big fruit-covered thing? I mean, how were other people supposed to know you were going to do that? I could have done that if I'd known. I thought we had to draw a bonnet."

"It's weird, isn't it?" says Joshua. "It's as if you can be *rewarded* for actually *having an imagination*."

"Yeah!" scoffs Harriet (not getting where he is coming from at all). "But luckily, only with Easter eggs." And then she saunters off.

Oh my God. I think I might have found a person I hate more than Amelia! And I never thought that was possible. Harriet is *annoyed* I've beaten her. Even though she wins everything all the time, she still wants all the prizes and can't be happy for other people. She has to pretend they *cheated,* rather than worked hard.

For a moment I'm seething, and then I realise this means she must be kind of unhappy. Plus, I remember that I am being positive about everything from now on, so I don't need to worry about this.

Natalie and Amelia and me all get the bus home together at the end of school.

I feel kind of pleased with myself. I mean, I know that Amelia feels like she beat me because of the spelling bee and everything, but I sort of feel like *I won*, because my cartoons are doing so well, and because, well, in a way, they both *came crawling back*, wanting to be my friend. (I mean, I know that isn't entirely what happened. But that is kind of what happened.)

Plus, it is Friday night! So we can have even more fun! I'm going to go home to get changed, then we are all meeting up round Natalie's, and then we are going to go out to McDonald's! Life is good.

As I arrive home, my mum is chatting to the VanDerks over the hedge again.

"Mum! Mum! I'm going to go to Natalie's! That's OK, isn't it?"

My mum arches an eyebrow curiously, but doesn't comment any further on how Natalie is suddenly back in my life.

"Any news on the drawing competition?" asks Mr VanDerk smugly and importantly.

"Why didn't you tell me you were entering a drawing competition?" asks my mum then, suddenly looking weary.

"Hang on, you mean Harriet hasn't told you?" I ask.

"Oh, she's not back yet, she's at *advanced maths*," says Mrs VanDerk proudly.

"Oh, right," I say. *Wow*. This family are so used to winning everything that they are totally *assuming* they have won again. They don't know I beat Harriet yet.

I have no idea what that kind of blinkered self-confidence must feel like. (I wonder briefly if it would be *good*, or if it would inevitably make life quite disappointing.)

"So? How did everybody do?" probes Mr VanDerk.

"Oh. Well, actually, I won. Mum, can I go to Natalie's, please?"

"Sorry, what did you say? It sounded like you said you won?" says Mrs VanDerk.

I feel like I'm getting bored with this conversation. I want to get changed and get to Natalie's. "Yes, I won. I won the whole thing. I won the first prize. I beat everybody in 6P and 6C." (They stare at me.) "Harriet was a runner-up," I add. "Now can I please go to Natalie's?"

"*Did you?*" My mum sounds incredulous.

"Yeah, look, this is my prize." I show them the giant Easter egg. "Harriet's got a smaller one," I say to the VanDerks.

"Oh, well done, Jessica!" My mum gives me a massive hug.

"Will you drive me to Natalie's?" I ask.

"Of course! You know, we should celebrate," says my mum. Then, almost as an aside, she adds quietly to me, "I knew you two would sort things out if I just left you to it. Girls can be so funny at your age." (Which I think (a) is ludicrous, seeing as my mum did try to interfere at least once; and (b) totally undermines my intense and moving struggle.)

"Oh well." Mr VanDerk turns to Mrs VanDerk, trying to sound nonchalant. "It's only a drawing competition."

My mum loosens her third embrace of me, and faces the VanDerks. "But, just the other day, you were saying there was no such thing as *only*," she says. "You said an achievement was an achievement, and it was always something to be proud of. I thought they were lovely stirring words to encourage children. You shouldn't take them back, it might get confusing."

"Oh, no, of course. It is, it is an achievement," blusters Mr VanDerk. "Absolutely. And well done." And with that, the VanDerks shuffle back into their house.

"Mum, you really shouldn't gloat," I say, when they're gone.

"I don't know what you're talking about, darling," says my mum, leading me back into the house with a big smile on her face.

"Why is Mum so happy?" asks Ryan as we enter

the house. He and my dad are sitting at the kitchen table and look up at us.

"Oh, did you tell Jess the good news?" asks my dad.

"What good news?" demands Ryan.

It starts to feel a bit like my family are playing that game where you have to answer a question with another question.

"Well," says my dad, smiling. "As of now, we are no longer on an economy drive!"

"Yeeeeeeeeeeeeeeeessssssssss!" shouts Ryan, jumping up and running round the table. "Pizza! Pizza! Pizza!" he chants as he runs. Then he stops dead as another thought occurs to him. "*Kit Kats*," he breathes in wonder.

My parents laugh at Ryan earnestly proclaiming Kit Kats the holy grail of his cuisine-based ambition. I manage a chuckle. He does look quite cute.

I nearly make a cheeky comment about how it was about time, because otherwise we would have been really scraping the barrel. And then eating the barrel. But looking at their happy faces, I decide not to. Let them have their fun. Plus, I'm super happy myself now – I'm going to Natalie's!

200

Ah, life is good. I'm sitting in McDonald's with Natalie and Amelia, eating a McFlurry, and we are discussing  the future. In general. Mainly they seem to want to organise a trip involving the basketball team, but the point is, we all have this joint future together.

"So, should we do actual invites?" asks Natalie. "Or would that make boys *not* want to do something?"

"I think classy boys would respond well to invites," insists Amelia.

Oh my God, is this what they have been doing all this time without me? Discussing whether boys do or don't like invites? Because if it is, I really haven't missed that much.

"What do you think, Jess?" asks Natalie. "What do you think would make boys want to go somewhere?"

"Um … just fun stuff, I guess," I reply.

"Well, *duh*," says Amelia tiredly. "We *know* that. Care to be more specific?"

"Uh … like … Thorpe Park or something …" I offer.

"Great idea!" beams Natalie.

Amelia looks annoyed. "Well, I think we should make a list of suggestions and then vote on the best ones." (OK, so, seriously. Have I really just missed a load of admin all this time?)

"Or, we could do Rock Paper Scissors?" suggests Natalie. (Yes, yes it is. I've just missed out on admin.)

"Hey, or we could do Rock Paper Scissors to decide whether to do Rock Paper Scissors," I joke.

"OK," says Amelia seriously.

Ohh. OK, I still might hate Amelia. But it doesn't matter, because I've got Natalie back, and later we are going to go back to her house and have a sleepover and watch a programme about dinosaurs together.

Life is good.